OUT OF THE SHADOWS

A Vintage Creasey

OUT OF

A FALCON'S HEAD MYSTERY

THE WORLD PUBLISHING COMPANY

THE SHADOWS

John Creasey

AS MICHAEL HALLIDAY

New York and Cleveland

Published by The World Publishing Company
First American Edition
First printing—1971

Library of Congress catalog card number: 73-148409
Printed in the United States of America

WORLD PUBLISHING
TIMES MIRROR

CONTENTS

1

HOMECOMING

THE night was calm and quiet. A gentle wind stirred the leaves of the beech tree which grew near a corner of the house, pressed caressingly against the closed heads of tulips and the pale petals of daffodils, and murmured among the wallflowers in beds near the house and on either side of the short, gravel drive. The wind touched the smooth lawns, stole quietly towards the back of the house, was halted by the beech hedge which hid the kitchen garden, and rustled its brittle brown leaves.

The stars were out but there was no moon.

Four people lay sleeping in the house; man and wife together in a double bed from which, by day, they could see the tiny, bright green leaves of the trees waking in this golden spring. Their daughter was in an adjoining room, overlooking the front lawns, the drive and flowers—and distant woods, which were broken here and there by the roof of a house. Their guest, who might one day become their son-in-law, was in a room across the landing from these two, with pleasant views. The fourth bedroom was empty.

It was after five o'clock; dawn would soon come, and the new day with its hope, its promise and its disappointments.

A sound broke the quiet.

It came from the road which served this house and a dozen near by, a little colony a mile from Lingham, ten miles from Minchester, in the middle of Linshire's broad acres.

A cyclist approached; tyres jolted over the uneven surface of the unmade road. It was a youth, and his gasping breath made more noise than the tyres, for the road led uphill. He stopped by the gates of the house and stood leaning against his machine, fighting for breath. Then he looked behind him. Just in sight, at the corner with the main road, a lamp burned brightly; no shadow appeared against it, and he could hear no other sound.

He wheeled the bicycle to the gates, opened one, thrust the bicycle through and then closed the gate stealthily behind him. His breathing was quieter but no less troubled. He staggered once and the bicycle nearly fell; he saved it, making a scratching sound on the loose gravel. Between this garden and the one next door was a row of beech trees, but the youth could see through the branches. A light went on at the neighbour's house, fifty or sixty yards away. It shone brightly, the only light now visible. He stared at it as he pushed the machine towards the house, past the beech tree at the corner, and round to the back. He leaned it against the wall of a wooden garage, then staggered away.

After a moment's rest, he walked slowly towards the back of the house. He could just make out the shapes of the windows. Reaching the nearest, he groped round the frame, trying to open it. It was tightly closed; so were the others at the back, another at the side.

His footsteps made little noise, he walked cautiously, fearfully. When he reached the far side of the house, he knew that none of the downstairs windows was open, there was no way in through them. Slowly, with dragging footsteps, he went to the front door, which was protected by a porch. He stepped into the porch and leaned against the wall, still breathing hard; exhausted. The bell-push was near his right hand; he had only to stretch out and press it and a bell would ring in the kitchen, another upstairs.

He was taken by a sudden fit of shivering.

Soon, he moved wearily away from the porch and went towards the beech tree, looking up at the branches where they hid the stars, and to the window of the room where his parents slept. That was open. Years ago, to scare his mother, he had climbed the tree and edged his way along a bending bough, hoping to get through the window, but it was out of reach. He gazed longingly at the branch which might now support him, but knew that he would not be able to climb up. His left shoulder hurt badly; it burned.

He bent down, picked up a handful of gravel, hesitated, then threw it at the window. It rattled sharply. He waited tensely, hoping to hear his mother or his father move, but there was no sound. He bent down for more gravel; most of this struck the wall, not the window, but almost before the sound had died, he heard his mother's voice.

"George! George, wake up." The words came clearly, sharpened by alarm. "George!"

In the quiet night, the youth heard other noises, rustling and creaking, followed by his father's voice, gruff and indistinct. The woman's came again, but this time her words did not travel far. After more creaking followed, there was another rumble from the man. Then the woman's voice came clearly.

"I tell you I heard something!"

The youth picked up more gravel, and tossed it upwards. As it struck the glass, his mother gasped so loudly that he felt like screaming: "Quiet, keep quiet!"

"Don't upset yourself," his father said, "I'll see what it is." He was nearer the window, must have got out of bed very quietly. "It's all right, my dear." That was the familiar patient voice which his father often used with his mother; a voice the youth detested.

He heard the window move up, and could just make out the shape of his father's head and shoulders. A moment later a light went on in the room, showing the older man clearly, his big shoulders in striped pyjamas.

"Who's that?"

"Dad," the youth whispered. "Let me in. Hurry."

"Bob!"

"Don't shout! Let me in."

"George, *what* did you say? Is that *Robert*?" The woman's voice was sharp and clear. "Oh, thank God!"

"Hurry," the youth pleaded. "Hurry, Dad."

"Go to the front door," his father called down quietly. "I won't be a minute."

The head and shoulders vanished from sight but the youth did not move immediately. His mother appeared against the light, her fair hair like a crown.

"Oh, Robert, where have you been, what have you—"

"*Please be quiet!*"

The urgency of the boy's tone silenced her, perhaps passed on a little of his fear. She leaned out to watch him as he went slowly towards the front door. He was there before his father. Soon the bolts were drawn and the door opened. Light shone into the garden and on the youth's dark hair and pale face, on to the deep bleeding cut in his neck and the blood that had dried on his coat and collar.

Shock leapt into the older man's eyes, but George Canning did not speak, just stepped aside. As his son crossed the threshold, he put out a hand to help him.

"Dad, I—"

"It's all right, Bob, take it easy." The gruff voice tried vainly to be reassuring. George put an arm round his son's shoulder, closed the door with his free hand, then turned and helped Bob along the wide passage.

Belle Canning appeared at the half-landing, wearing only a filmy nightdress, big blue eyes rounded in a face that might have been made of china. When she saw the blood, her mouth opened; she raised both hands but only a thin sound came from her lips.

"Quiet," croaked her son despairingly. "Don't wake—"

Canning felt him crumple, and saved him from falling. Belle stood quite still, her mouth wide open. Canning, a big man, supported the youth until he was able to put a hand beneath his knees, another round his shoulders, and lift him.

"Don't talk, Belle. Be quiet. Get the first-aid box from the bathroom." He talked as if he were giving orders to a child. Perhaps it was the tone of his voice which made her relax and turn away. She faltered as she reached the landing, then went slowly towards the bathroom.

Canning carried his son into the large bedroom, and laid him on the bed. He stared down. The absolute stillness of the features made the pale face look worse; Bob might have been at death's door. The gash in his cheek was ugly and blood smeared his forehead as well as his chin. There was blood on his hands. He wore a light grey suit that was also smeared, and brown shoes. His tie had been pulled to one side, his collar was rucked up, but his black hair was brushed sleekly back from his forehead.

"Oh, God, what's happened to him, what's happened?" Belle moaned as she put the big white box on the bedside table heavily, then clutched Cannings' arm. "George, is he dead? Is he—"

"Of course not," Canning said sharply. "Pull yourself together. Close the door—*quietly*."

She began to tremble, clutching him convulsively.

"Is he dead?" she gasped.

"He's no more dead than you are," Canning said. He forced her hand away, took her shoulders and shook her. "Be quiet, and pull yourself together. He doesn't want the others to know he's here. Close the door, then go and wet your sponge and bring it to me. With a towel. Understand? He needs your help."

She looked at her son again, then turned towards the hand basin in a corner of the room. Canning opened the first-aid box, took out cotton wool, a small bottle of Dettol and some oddments. He didn't quite know what to do, the wound looked so ugly. Finally, he spread the towel over Bob's chest and began to bathe the cut.

"Mix some Dettol," he said. "Not too strong. Then put the kettle on, and get your hot-water bottle."

She moved off in a daze, glancing at Bob, then closing her eyes as if to shut out the vision.

Canning sponged the wound gently. He had a strong, rugged face, with heavy greying eyebrows, thick grey hair, a short, broad nose and a large mouth. His lips were set tightly. Gradually the congealed blood was cleaned away and the cut was revealed—about an inch long and just below the cheek-bone. It wasn't really so bad.

Belle came back.

"Shall I get some brandy? Yes, I'll get some." She moved towards the door.

"Not yet," Canning said. "Is the kettle on?"

"Of course it is," she said with sullen tartness. "I can't *make* it boil. And I'm going to get some brandy." She hurried out of the room, leaving the door open. She didn't make much noise, but Canning could hear her going down the stairs. She wasn't likely to disturb the others if they hadn't been disturbed already. He wished he could see their doors. He went across to the basin and squeezed out the sponge; the white porcelain was smeared with red.

When he reached the bedside, Bob's eyes were flickering. Canning dabbed the wound again; no, it didn't look too bad. He put a gauze dressing on the wound but didn't fasten it down; first aid wasn't his best subject by a long way.

In a few minutes Bob ought to be able to explain what had happened, why he was so anxious not to wake the others.

It would be a bad business, Canning was sure. He was cursed with a neurotic wife and a bad son. Bad? Or weak?

Whatever had happened it was going to be an upsetting day; even if it was not so ominous as it looked, Belle would hover between hysteria and querulousness, there would be little opportunity to work. One part of his mind told him that he was being callous, but if one thing didn't disturb a day, another did; he wasn't so much callous as embittered.

Belle came back.

"How is he? I've got the—*Robert*! Look, his eyes are opening, he's coming round." She rushed to the bed and dropped down on her knees, seizing Bob's right hand. "Robert, it's your mother! Tell me what's happened, who did this dreadful thing to you."

She hadn't closed the door.

Canning went to it. There was no light under Celia's door, or Matthew's. He closed this one, quietly, and turned to look at his wife as she stared into Bob's half-open eyes. He was moistening his lips with his tongue. Canning took Belle's dressing-gown from the back of a chair and draped it round her shoulders, then put on his own. Belle was still talking nonsense; drivel. He half filled a glass with water and took it to the bedside.

"Mind, Belle." He put the glass on the bedside table, sat sideways on the bed and slid his arm beneath Bob's shoulders. "Sit up, Bob, I'll give you a drink."

Bob began to sit up, and winced.

"My—my shoulder hurts."

"Who *did* this to you?" demanded Belle shrilly. "He'll suffer for it, I promise you that!"

"Which shoulder?" Canning asked.

"The left."

"Well, try to sit up." Canning managed to raise him. "Go round the other side and push a pillow behind his back, Belle." For once she obeyed without arguing, and he put the glass to Bob's lips. "Like a cup of tea, Bob?"

"I—I would, rather."

"Give him some *brandy*," Belle insisted.

"Yes, all right." But Belle hadn't brought a spoon. Canning fetched one from the cupboard beneath the hand-basin, filled it and held it to Bob's lips. Bob's eyes were narrowed against the light. He looked grey and obviously he was in pain, was not just putting this on.

"Now let me have a look at that shoulder," Canning said. Even when he looked, he wouldn't be much wiser. "Can we get your coat off?"

"I'll try," Bob set his lips. Between them, they slid the coat over his left shoulder, then got it right off. There was no blood. "It's not so bad as I thought it would be, but—"

"I'll cut the sleeve," his mother said quickly. "Just a minute. Don't touch him, George." She hurried to the dressing-table and pulled open a drawer, rummaged for the scissors. At times she was surprisingly competent, at others, helpless; it depended on her mood. She cut the sleeve off; beneath the shirt Bob wore a grubby singlet.

The shoulder looked slightly swollen; when Canning prodded it gently, Bob winced again.

"Quicker we can get a doctor for that the better," Canning said. "What's the time?" He glanced at the clock on the mantelpiece; it was half-past five. "I think we can wait an hour or two, then—"

"I don't want a doctor," Bob said tautly. "You mustn't send for one."

There was fear as well as pain in his eyes; fear which alarmed Canning more than the physical injuries.

"Why not?" he asked. "What's the trouble, Bob?"

Belle had moved away from the bed, as if she too were touched by fear; and they watched their son.

2

CONFESSION

Bob closed his eyes and screwed up his face. Canning glanced at Belle and she looked away from the boy. Their eyes met in a moment of understanding; dread of the coming disclosure brought them together in a way that had once been common and yet precious; and a way which had almost been forgotten. Belle didn't move, but looked back at Bob.

His eyes were still closed, he moistened his lips again.

The electric kettle began to spout steam.

"Better make the tea," Canning said. "Or shall I do it?"

"No, I will."

"All right. Take it easy, Bob," Canning went on. "Like a cigarette?"

"Please." The word was only just audible.

Canning went to his coat, draped over a chair, took out a cigarette case and lighter, lit a cigarette and leaned across the bed to put it in his son's lips. He was now near Belle. She had filled the hot-water bottle and made the tea; teapot, cups and saucers, milk and sugar, had been put ready for the morning. She was quite calm; Canning didn't care to guess how long that would last.

"I'll let it brew a minute."

"Yes." Canning put his arm round her shoulders; she

had slipped into the dressing-gown and fastened the sash. She had a slim waist; at forty-four, there wasn't a woman anywhere with a better figure, and the older she got, the more she looked like a fragile china doll. "Put plenty of sugar into Bob's cup, and have a cup yourself," he went on, as he lit a cigarette, drew on it, and watched his son. Bob was pulling much too fiercely at his and his lips were trembling as if at any moment he might burst into tears. What in heaven's name had he done?

Belle poured out and took Bob his tea.

"Thanks," Bob took the cup from the saucer she held, and sipped. He looked very young. Since sipping the brandy, he had a better colour, but he wasn't warm enough. Canning took his coat from the back of the chair and draped it round Bob's shoulders; then he switched on the electric fire, and went across and closed the windows. When he had finished, Bob put the cup down.

"I don't want any more."

"Oh, just a *little* more, darling, it'll do you good."

"I—"

"Drink it up," Canning commanded.

Bob picked the cup up again, meekly, finished the tea, then leaned back on the pillows. He didn't close his eyes this time, but looked from his mother to his father, then back to his mother as if he knew that he could rely only on her for sympathy. There were tears in his eyes. Weak was the right word for him, Canning knew; not spineless—weak, wilful and stubborn.

"Robbie, darling, you *must* tell us what's happened?" Belle went back to the nursery name. "We'll understand, don't be worried about that. Whatever it is, we'll understand."

Canning stood quite still, all his fears storming. He felt that he could strike his son if he didn't begin to talk to explain. His hands were clenched, his mouth tightly shut.

"I broke into a house," Bob muttered. He closed his eyes again, as if he couldn't bear to look at them. "I know I was a fool, but—"

"*Robert!*"

"For God's sake don't scream at me! It's bad enough as it is, my shoulder's hurting like hell, my face—"

"Just tell us what happened, Bob." Canning kept his voice steady, didn't even sound unfriendly; but he knew now that everything he feared was going to be justified. "Until we know, we can't help, can we? Don't get excited. What house did you break into?"

"A—house in Minchester. I thought—" The boy broke off, drew deeply at the cigarette, then blurted out: "I thought everyone was out!"

"Why did you do it, Bob?" At least Belle was keeping quiet; perhaps at last she had been shocked into seeing wrong by her adored Robert.

"I—was broke. If you'd let me have that fifty pounds it would have been all right, but—" Bob stopped.

Canning didn't say anything about the fifty pounds; Bob had asked for it three weeks ago, and had stormed out of the house when he'd been refused. He hadn't been back until now. Mention of the money would begin the battle with Belle all over again; he'd driven *her* son away.

"Why pick on that particular house?"

"I knew the people," Bob muttered. "I knew they always kept money about, I thought it would be easy. I'd got in through a window and found some money in a cupboard. I was coming away when he—"

The words quavered. He stopped and screwed up his eyes again. Canning felt the gripping coldness of dread; what had followed, what could be worse than this?

"Oh, Robert, oh, my boy!" Belle whispered.

"Bob, I want you to tell me exactly what happened," Canning said very calmly. "We must know everything. You were leaving the house when a man appeared. What then?"

"He—he had a knife."

"Oh, it's dreadful," Belle said hoarsely. "I can't stand it."

"I thought he was going to kill me!" The words came out with shrill insistence. "He sprang at me from behind a door with the knife in his hand, that's when—that's when he cut my face. I kicked him, and he dropped the knife. We—we had—we fought for it. It was terrible. He got a grip on my arm, I thought he would pull it off, but—but I got away."

He stopped again. His mother said nothing, but her pallor was even greater than his. Canning stood picturing the scene and fearing what would follow, feeling a dread such as he had never known before.

"What happened to the other man?"

"I knocked him out."

"How?"

"I pushed him when I'd got my arm free, and tripped him up. He fell against a chair, and didn't get up. I rushed away. I didn't think I'd ever escape. My arm—"

"What happened to the money?"

"I dropped it, it's still in the house." Bob looked nervously, fearfully, at his father, holding the stub of the cigarette, biting his lips.

"How did you get here?"

"George—" Belle began.

"Just a minute. How did you get here?"

"I'd borrowed a bike! I wasn't coming here, first of all. I—I was so scared. I hid in a barn. Then I thought—I thought you'd help me." It was almost piteous.

"Who did you borrow the bike from?"

"I—"

"George, I won't allow you to worry him any more, you can see he's in dreadful pain." Belle stood up, abruptly. "We've got to find a way to help him. Robert, don't worry, we'll be able to do something. We must."

"I want to know where that bicycle came from," Canning said inexorably. "I want to know everything. What about it, Bob?"

"Oh, all right. I—I pinched it."

"Where from?"

"It was in a yard near my digs. Where I'd been staying."

"Where is it now?"

"Outside, if it hadn't been for the bike I'd never have got away!"

"What about the people at these 'digs' you talk about?"

"They—they didn't expect me back, I said I was going straight on to London!"

"We must let him rest," Belle broke in. She stood protectingly by the side of the bed, holding Bob's hand. "This has got to stop." Her voice was reedy, as if she expected opposition and intended to fight to get her own way this time. Canning looked from her to the boy, then moved for the first time, stubbed out his cigarette and took the end of Bob's from him.

"We've several things to decide before anyone can rest," he said reasoningly. He made another gauze pad, placed it on Bob's cheek and strapped it with adhesive tape. "Bob doesn't want Celia or Matthew to know about this, naturally, but they'll have to know he's home. That shoulder needs attention, too." He was only expressing part of what was in his mind. This affair couldn't be covered up, they couldn't keep Bob here for long without telling the police. That struggle with Belle would come soon, but he wasn't prepared to face it yet. He was not ready to face the fact that his only son had turned thief, deliberately broken into the house of a family he knew, to rob them; Canning wanted to hide from that ugly truth but would not be able to for long. "How does your shoulder feel now, Bob?"

"It—it's a bit better."

"I think we'll help him to his own room. We can tell the others that he came back late and is sleeping in. That will give us time to think. Take the hot-water bottle into his room, Belle, I'll bring him along. Be very quiet."

Canning was entering into a conspiracy which he knew could not last long. Belle was the danger, a far greater danger than Bob. After this, Bob would surely realize that unless he stopped behaving so wildly, he would become an outcast. True, he showed no sign of it yet, only of self-pity. But he was exhausted, and sick with pain. This could be the making of him.

Canning knew that he was forcing his thoughts along the channels in which he wanted them to go.

"I mustn't see them yet," Bob said hoarsely. "You can say I'm ill, keep them out of my room. I've got to lie low."

"You go and fix his bed," Canning said to Belle.

"Don't start on him again, George. Do you hear me?"

"I won't."

Belle clutched the hot-water bottle as she went out, opening the door very quietly and leaving it ajar. Canning moved to the side of the bed and sat down heavily. Bob wanted to evade his eyes but couldn't; Canning stared into the pale, frightened face and the bloodshot eyes.

"It's a mess, Bob, isn't it?"

"Yes. I know. I—I'm damned sorry."

"We'll see what we can do to help. About this fellow you knocked out—are you sure it's no worse than that?"

"He just banged his head against the chair."

"Did you have a look at him, to find out how bad it was?"

Bob hesitated. "I—no, I didn't, I just ran off."

Canning stood up. "Oh, well, we'll talk about it later. I'll pour you out another cup of tea, and get you some aspirins. They'll ease your shoulder." He went to the tray, and Bob was sipping the tea when Belle came back, looking at them suspiciously. She seemed satisfied that Bob hadn't been harassed.

"Any lights on in the other rooms?" Canning asked.

"No."

"Good. Ready, Bob." Canning moved to help.

"Mind his shoulder."

"I'll be careful."

In practice, it was not so difficult as he had expected. Canning kept his arm round the boy's waist, but Bob was able to move freely, although he kept his left shoulder fairly stiff. The electric fire burned brightly in the bedroom which Bob had left three weeks ago, in that fit of temper and disappointment. The bed was turned down, the bottle in a green cover just showed against the sheets. Canning helped his son in.

"Try to sleep."

"All right, Dad. And—thanks."

"Yes." Canning went out, glanced at the other doors, and saw a light under Matthew's. He stood quite still, listening. He heard nothing.

Dawn's grey light was creeping over the sky and into the house; the landing window faced east, showing the dimming stars. Canning went back to Bob's room, and whispered:

"Be very quiet, Matthew's awake." He went out again, hesitated, then stood by Matthew's door. He had never been happy about having Matthew Grant to "dig" here, but Belle had insisted. There were advantages: money was tight and getting tighter, and Matthew paid adequately even generously, for his keep. But he was in love with Celia and most certainly Celia was in love with him. Was it wise to throw them together, to give them opportunity after opportunity to be on their own? Canning had nothing against Matthew, in fact rather liked him—as well as he could like anyone who meant to marry Celia.

She was everything that Bob was not.

Belle had wanted the extra money, of course, but that wasn't her only motive. Having Matthew here would keep Celia at home more. It was working out; nothing had gone wrong during the four months since Matthew had come, but Canning wasn't easy in his mind. As with many things he didn't like, he took the line of least resistance. That could not dispel his uneasiness.

The bed creaked in Matthew's room.

Belle came out of Bob's, and closed the door softly; but the lock clicked faintly. She came towards Canning, making hardly a sound.

"What are you going to do?" The whisper was close to his ear, he felt her warm breath.

"Go back to our room, we'll make up some story later."

The great danger was past—that Matthew should come out while Bob's door was open. It wasn't going to be easy lying to Matthew; he had a disconcerting frankness, a candour and quality of honesty that one had to admire.

"Come on." They went back, but hadn't reached the door of their room before Matthew's opened.

He called: "Everything all right?"

Belle started violently. Canning pushed her forward lightly, and turned, managed to smile, and said:

"Yes. Bob came home unexpectedly."

"Oh, good!"

"My wife's rather upset, do you mind if we talk about it later?"

"Whenever you like." Matthew had a square face, and a quick smile which showed good teeth. "I thought I heard something. Now that I know I won't disturb you, I'll go down and make myself a cup of tea."

"Good idea. Don't disturb Bob, will you."

"No one will hear a sound," Matthew promised. He returned to his room, and Canning went into his and closed the door. Belle was back in bed, sitting up with both the pillows behind her. She looked helplessly young and pretty, with her little tilted nose and rumpled curls; she still wore her dressing-gown. "He's gone down to make himself some tea, he didn't suspect anything." Canning went across to the dressing-table and lit another cigarette. Outside, the birds were beginning to call, soon the morning chorus would be at its height; he seldom heard it. The daylight was bright enough for him to see the massed trees in the distance, the roofs of other houses, as well as the drive and the lawn. "Can I get you anything?"

"My head's dreadful."

"Have a couple of aspirins and try to relax for a bit. It's a nasty mess, but—"

"George," Belle said very clearly, "we must help Bob. It was a wicked thing to do, I know, but he *is* our son. What are you thinking of doing? It's no use talking about resting, we've got to decide."

This was when he ought to say that they must tell the police. Perhaps Belle suspected that he would think that, and was preparing for the fight. He had to make her understand that the police would find out, beyond any doubt, that it would be folly to try to hide Bob. But need he start now? He hadn't liked the look of Bob's shoulder, it would probably be necessary to send for the doctor soon; and that would be a better time to talk.

He was standing undecided when he heard the squeak of Celia's door. Both turned their heads sharply and stared, expecting their door to open or Celia to tap. Neither thing happened. They heard no sound, and exchanged puzzled glances. Canning moved round the bed, and opened the door. There was no light in either Matthew's or Celia's room. Then he heard Matthew say quietly:

"Hallo, darling! You up, too? Wonderful."

"Everyone seemed to be moving about, I'm glad it was only you." There was a laugh in Celia's voice; gaiety came easily to her. Next moment, a door downstairs closed and Canning heard nothing more.

"She's gone down to Matthew," he said.

"I've got ears. Never mind them, what are we—" Belle broke off, her hands rising to her throat with a clutching gesture. "George! That bicycle's outside, they mustn't see it."

3

THE TELEPHONE CALL

THERE was horror in Belle's eyes; or she wanted Canning to think there was. He knew only too well how she acted, playing on his nerves, trying every trick to get her own way. Watching her, he believed that this was real. She had thought of the bicycle and the story of its theft, knew what it might lead to. There had never been any doubt about what she would do; at all costs she would try to hide Bob from the police, do everything she could to make sure that he was never found out. She had a quick mind; she was a termagant at times, a scold, and towards him often vicious whenever he really upset her; but she wasn't a fool.

"Don't be silly," Canning said. He sat down in the armchair over which his coat was draped. "Even if they see it, they won't know where it came from. They won't know that Bob stole it." He used the word 'stole' deliberately, but it had no outward effect on her. "We shan't help if we get hysterical about it."

Belle lowered her hands, slowly.

"I'd rather get rid of the bicycle."

"I don't see how we can."

"You could wheel it across to the woods, and hide it there," she said. "Or push it into the quarry. Don't you want to help him?"

"I'm trying to decide the best way. Let's try to keep calm about this, Belle. We've always known that he was kicking over the traces. He's stolen from us and from Celia, and we weren't severe enough with him. Sooner or later something like this was bound to happen. Now we've to make up our minds what will really help him most. I'm not sure that shielding him will."

Belle didn't comment, but just stared. Her blue eyes might have been made of china, too, they were so cold. There was no warmth in her for Canning. Years ago, something had frozen all the feeling she had once had for him, and over the twenty long years she had grown icier. Canning had tried to find out the cause, so as to melt the ice in her, but given it up except for occasional, impulsive efforts.

There were still fierce, passionate outbursts between them, the call of body to body; but even allowing for those they led a strange, unnatural life. There were a few compensations of a kind. He had the garden, his work and some outside interests, and Belle seldom interfered with them. There was Celia; gay, lovely Celia. He and Belle had many things in common, too. They enjoyed the same kind of music, the same films, the same plays and—oddly, liked the same people. Belle was house-proud and thrifty to a fault, stretching a pound much further than most of their neighbours.

Whenever his bitterness raged within him, Canning would try to remind himself of all those things.

Now he saw the icy blue of her eyes, expected an outburst, hoped that she would not shout loudly enough to be heard downstairs. He need not have feared. She spoke quietly and with great deliberation.

"Of course we are going to shield him. We shall help him to get away from here, if necessary. It may not be necessary. There is no reason why the police should connect him with —the trouble at that house. Probably they never will. I shall nurse him back to health and then you will find work for him. You can easily find him another position among all your friends. I know you've refused to try again, because of his mistakes, but now you're going to help him. You're going to behave as a father should behave."

Canning said painfully: "Belle, he broke into a house, to steal. Don't you understand what that means? It was deliberate crime. He left a man there, unconscious, and was so callous that he didn't trouble to find out if he were really hurt. He's quite beyond us. I've tried—"

"You haven't tried," Belle said in the same scornful, deliberate way. "You've never tried to understand him. From now on, you will."

"Belle, what's the use of pretending? Bob needs a sharp lesson, to make him realize that he can't go on being pampered. I've indulged you too much about Bob, against my better judgment. I can't indulge you over this. God knows what we've done to deserve a rogue for a son, but—"

He saw the glitter flash into her eyes. She swung her arm, snatched a cup from the tray and flung it at him. It went wide, hit the curtain and fell to the carpet. The handle came off, while the tea dregs dripped slowly from the curtain. She snatched at another cup, white Canning sat quite still, watching her. She made as if to throw it, but didn't. She nursed the cup in her hand. He thought she would start screaming; instead, she kept silent, brooding as their eyes met in challenge. At last, Canning stood up and moved towards the door. Before he reached it, she said:

"George, listen to me."

He turned to look at her, and did not like the glitter in her eyes or the vicious twist of her lips.

"We are going to protect Bob. We're not going to let them send him to prison. If you do anything to help the police find out he was at that house last night, I'll kill you. Do you understand? I'll kill you."

Before she finished, Canning was on the landing. He leaned against the wall staring at Matthew's door, which was ajar, and the bathroom which was by the head of the stairs. He went slowly to the bathroom, sat on the edge of the pale green bath and looked into the green-framed mirror. His stubble was more grey than his hair, and he badly needed a shave. He studied the reflection of the strong face, which he knew was a sham. There was no moral courage in him. Why should he wonder at Bob's weakness?

The deep lines across his forehead and at his mouth, and a criss-cross of crowsfeet at his eyes, told their own story. He was forty-seven and he looked in the middle fifties; his own weakness was partly responsible for that.

He had given way to Belle a thousand times, but how could he give way over this? It cut across every principle he claimed to believe in. Her charge that he had not tried to help Bob had no sting because it wasn't true. He had talked, argued, guided by example; he had punished sharply when words had proved useless. He had failed, of course, and that was mostly Belle's fault. She had always shielded Bob, explaining all his faults away. He was young, he mixed with the wrong set, there was no real vice in him—any excuse served her purpose. The truth was quite simple; she was quite blind to her son's faults, his vices, his lies. She doted.

The threat to kill was no more than a measure of the intensity of her feeling. She always talked wildly when they quarrelled, especially over Bob. And she often had her way. When he had been dismissed from his work twice within a few months, each time for pilfering, she had persuaded George to use his influence with the employers, who were his friends, not to prosecute. He'd done that twice, then put his foot down. He had not found Bob work with friends again, and she had resented that bitterly.

Bob had gambled for years; that had started at school. It was the root of the trouble. His spell in the Army hadn't helped him. He had dropped into an 'easy billet', and wasted even those years. Since then he had lived at home until three weeks ago. He had pretended to look for a job, actually loafed, or at the most convenient race meeting, or with cronies playing pitch and toss, billiards or cards, always any game with money at stake. He was never interested in anything for long, but had crazes; now roller-skating or swimming or cycling; his latest had been a trumpet which he had wheedled out of his mother. There had been talk of setting up a dance band, but it had soon died down.

Two years ago, against Canning's wish, they had bought the boy a motor-cycle. Belle had been on edge whenever he was out on it, yet had been determined to give him the machine. Five times in eighteen months he had been fined for ignoring traffic lights; and twice for speeding. After two endorsements, the Court had suspended his licence for six months.

Canning had ordered him to sell the machine, expecting trouble, but there had been no fight. Bob had said that he was fed up with it, anyhow; and Belle had been pleased. Canning never knew what the boy had done with the money; gambled it away, probably. He should have found out; he showed weakness after weakness, all to conciliate Belle.

She had really decided to take Matthew as a boarder so that she could give Bob pocket money; what she saved by thrift she would readily squander on their son.

Three weeks ago, Bob had been dunned for fifty pounds. He had asked Canning for it, and stormed out of the house when it had been refused. That time Canning had thought that Belle would really go off her head, but on the second day she had calmed down. That was because she had heard from Bob, of course; she had probably met him in Minchester without telling Canning and given him a few pounds;

but she hadn't persuaded him to come home. Bob had revolted against a discipline which had always been far too light.

How much could he blame himself? Canning wondered miserably.

He stirred. Sunlight was coming in at a corner of the window, a yellow shaft of beauty. The birds were quieter now, and busy. He opened the window and looked out over the smiling fields and the distant woods, where Belle thought he could take the bicycle. The quarry was in a different direction; west from here. He leaned further out, looking down and seeing the bicycle leaning against the wall, an old black machine someone was going to miss this morning.

He turned, took out his shaving gear, shaved carefully and then bathed. He must have been in the bathroom for half an hour. When he went out, Matthew's door was closed, Celia's open. He could see the shadow of her movements at the dressing-table.

She heard him.

"Is that you, Dad?"

"Up early, aren't you?" Canning managed to grin as his daughter leaned back on her dressing-table stool to look at him. She was combing her long, corn-coloured hair, which rippled down to her shoulders; he was always sorry that she put it up so often. She had her mother's colouring, fair clear skin and startlingly blue eyes, her mother's nose and chin, but Canning's mouth, wide and full of laughter.

"I must have heard Bob come in. What time did he arrive?"

Canning went in and kissed her forehead. She was wearing a shiny pink slip, with a towel round her shoulders.

"How did you know he was here?"

"Matt told me, we had a cup of tea in the kitchen. Something woke him up, too. We're going for a walk before breakfast!" She was eager, happy; at times he wondered if she were as completely oblivious of the strain between her parents as she appeared to be. Occasionally she seemed to make a form of peace between them, unwittingly. Looking at her as she leaned back, her breasts thrusting against the shiny pink, Canning could imagine that Matthew was as wildly in love with her as he had once been with Belle. Her eyes glowed. "Care to come?"

"I'll leave that to you youngsters. Don't be late for breakfast."

"I'm hungry already," Celia said, and swayed forward on the stool, nearer the mirror.

Canning went downstairs. Matthew was still in his room, so neither of them would notice him go out. He opened the back door, which led from the small, immaculate kitchen, and stepped into the crisp morning air. The bicycle was within arm's reach. He moved it, wheeling it to the end of the garage. There was room for it between the garage and the beech hedge, Matthew and Celia wouldn't notice it there. He went back, glanced at the kitchen clock and saw that it wasn't yet seven. Celia left for her office in Minchester at half-past eight, eight o'clock was the usual breakfast time. He felt hungry, and munched some biscuits, then put on a kettle. While waiting for it to boil, he started getting the breakfast things ready; it was something to do.

Matthew came downstairs first, saw him, and walked smilingly into the room.

"Restless this morning, sir?" The courtesy came easily and pleasantly, a little habit he would not drop. "Anything I can do to help?"

"No, thanks, Matt. Sorry we disturbed you."

"Couldn't have been better, Celia and I are going as far as the quarry and back," Matthew said.

He was nearly six feet tall, lean, almost thin, but with very wide shoulders. His square face had a spirited, confident look, and that also showed in his grey eyes. His hair, cut short, was between colours and grew well back from his wide forehead. In repose, he was good-looking; his smile gave him a touch of distinction; he had Celia's quality of zest, and appeared to enjoy most things in life. His grey tweed jacket sat well on him, and his grey flannels were newly creased; in fact he was always well dressed and wore his clothes with a casual air which suited him. He ran his own small business, an architect and surveyor with offices in Minchester; Celia worked in the same building with a firm of solicitors.

Celia came hurrying down, a short camel-hair coat flung over a dark green dress, her hair cascading to her shoulders.

"Ready, Matt?"

"Coming!"

"We'll be back by eight," Celia said. "I didn't disturb mother, as there wasn't a sound from the room." There was a question in her eyes which Canning preferred not to answer, a silent: 'Is everything all right?' It was at moments like these that he thought that Celia knew more than she let him know. She squeezed his hand as they went out by the kitchen door; if he hadn't moved the bicycle, they would have seen it.

They stepped out briskly.

The kettle began to boil. Canning turned from the door, made his tea, took it into the dining-room, and laid the table for breakfast.

Belle wasn't down by half-past seven. He didn't want to go and start the scene off again, it would be better to let her make the first move. He looked moodily out of the window to the back of the garage. By hiding the bicycle, he had begun the familiar, hated slide away from his convictions; but he wasn't going to give in, he had simply gained time. Perhaps he ought to go up at once and have it out. If there were going to be a screaming fit, it would matter less with Matthew and Celia out of the way.

He went upstairs.

The bedroom door opened as he reached the landing. Belle was still in her dressing-gown. He stood and waited. Then he saw that there was something different about her. She looked older, and her eyes were moist; soft. She seldom cried. She moved slowly forward, looking at him, and stretched out her hand, a gesture from the past. He took her fingers; squeezed.

"Let's go downstairs," she said, "Bob might be asleep."

Her voice was husky. Still holding hands, they went downstairs. Canning didn't know what to think, still felt surprised when they reached the kitchen. Normally Belle would have looked round and cried out with affected pleasure at the preparations for breakfast; now, she seemed to notice nothing.

"George, what are we going to do?" she asked as if helplessly. "What *can* we do?"

He didn't answer.

"I know you're right," Belle said. Her voice was lifeless. "I know what we ought to do, but—but can't we avoid it somehow? Isn't there any way we can make him understand that it's—it's his last chance? I just don't believe that he's really bad. He's been difficult, nothing's gone right, but—" she broke off, and sat on the painted wooden chair by the square enamel-topped table; there was despair in her. "Do the others—suspect anything?"

"I don't think so." Canning was almost at a loss for words. He didn't recognize Belle's mood but was suspicious of it in spite of an almost painful thrust of hope. She might have decided that this was the way to win him round—or might mean what she said. "They'll be back by eight," he added.

"I must start breakfast." Belle glanced at the clock but didn't move. "George, can't we wait until we know what happened, whether the man was hurt badly? He—he may not have recognized Bob. Will it do any harm to wait for a few hours? If he isn't badly hurt, and there's no reason why he should be, then the shock of all this might—might have the right effect on Bob. Will you wait?"

"I'm not sure that we ought to." Canning was gruff. He looked at her searchingly, trying to understand, wanting to believe. "Can I rely on you, Belle? To try to make him stop this nonsense, I mean, if he gets away with it this time? It's no use pretending, you haven't helped in the past."

This was usually enough to provoke an outburst; it didn't, now. She closed her eyes.

"I'll try," she whispered. "I love him so much, George. I can't explain why I feel so desperate, but—" she broke off again, and tears forced their way through her lashes. She had not seemed so helpless and dependent on Canning for so long that it was like looking at someone vaguely remembered. "I'll try," she repeated.

He moved towards her, a feeling of swift compassion, almost hope that she as well as Bob might have been shocked into realization of folly. Before he reached her, he stopped abruptly. Her eyes opened in sudden alarm and she stared towards the hall.

The telephone bell began to ring.

4

THE SUMMONS

CANNING turned to look into the hall. Belle stood up slowly, and joined him. The bell went on ringing. There hadn't been an early call like this for months; years. He felt as if the bell were ringing inside him, screeching alarm.

"Oh, no," Belle whispered. "Not already, no."

"It—may be a wrong number." Canning said the first thing that came into his head, although he felt sure that this was the police, that the man had recognized Bob. Who but the police would ring up so early? Belle obviously felt the same, and the possibility terrified her. Bob had left something behind, had been identified, somehow. The bell kept ringing, urgent, demanding. "I'll go." Canning made himself hurry into the hall. The telephone was on a small oak table outside the drawing-room door. He picked it up, while facing the kitchen, with Belle in the doorway. She had one hand against the wall for support.

"Hallo?"

A man said: "Is that Lingham 53?"

"Yes."

Belle took her hand away from the door; seemed to sway.

"Just a moment, please, I have a call for you."

Canning had to wait, and there was nothing he could say to help Belle. The light, coming through the open drawing-room door, was soft and kind to her, giving grace and almost beauty to her prettiness. How large her eyes were!

Another man said: "Is that Lingham 53?"

"Yes."

"I'm sorry to worry you, but is Mr. Matthew Grant there?'

"*Who?*"

"Matthew Grant. I'm awfully sorry to disturb you so early, but—"

"He—he's out at the moment," Canning said with an effort. The relief was so great that he felt light-headed. "Can I get him to ring you back?"

"Will you?" The man sounded anxious. "I'd be really grateful. Minchester 83341."

"Minchester 8—"

"Never mind the number, just tell him it's Jerry. I'd like him to call as soon as he comes in, it's extremely urgent."

"I'll tell him."

"Thanks very much. I'm sorry—"

"It doesn't matter. Good-bye." Canning put the receiver down slowly. Belle moved towards him as he jerked words out. "Someone for Matthew, nothing to worry about." She came on, swaying, and he realized that she looked ill, almost as ill as Bob had. She almost fell into his arms; he felt her shivering.

"I—I thought it was—" she didn't finish.

"I know. Look here, you'd better get back to bed." Canning was emphatic, and moved with her towards the stairs. "I'll get breakfast, that'll be no hardship. You must take it easier. We'll have to wait and see what happens."

That was the second defeat, coming swiftly upon the bicycle surrender. He recognized it without bitterness, because of this different Belle. She wasn't acting, this wasn't just to charm away his mood; of course, she was suffering from shock.

"Before you know where you are, you'll need a doctor, too." Canning went on. He helped her upstairs, and she didn't speak but leaned heavily on him. The bed was as they had left it, damp on one edge; for the first time he noticed that the sheet was stained a pale pink, near his side, from Bob's blood. He guided Belle to the other, and helped her into bed. "No, don't sit up, lie down. I'll manage. I'll tell the others you've got a headache, then they won't expect you down. I'll keep Celia out of the room, somehow."

He stood looking down at her. Her eyes were enormous, and she seemed flushed; he wondered if she had a temperature.

"Just try to rest." He moved away, but before he reached the door she called:

"George."

"Yes?" It was easier to smile at her.

"*Do* you hate him?"

"You get the damnedest ideas," Canning forced himself to say cheerfully. "Get that nonsense out of your head. He's beyond me sometimes, but—"

"You're sure you don't?"

"I suppose that's the trouble with you," Canning said gruffly: he couldn't keep the words back. "You just think I'm an unnatural father. I'll do the best I possibly can for him. Now try to rest."

He went out before she could speak again, and paused outside Bob's door. So Belle thought that he hated his son. He'd been nearer the truth when he had said that the boy was beyond him; he just didn't understand Bob. A throwback, perhaps, to someone in the family, her side or his, there were the reprobates in most families. But hate? No, it wasn't as strong as that.

He listened, heard nothing, and opened the door cautiously; there was still no sound. The curtains were drawn but they weren't lined, and there was plenty of light in the room.

Bob lay on his right side, facing the door, asleep. He looked quite peaceful. The face wound hadn't bled any more; not seriously, anyhow, the pad looked white. It was a sallow face with sharp, handsome features; that was another misfortune for Bob, he was too good-looking. Canning had expected that his first serious trouble would be over a girl. Sleeping, the nastiness of his expression did not show. He had very long dark eyelashes and big eyes; as large as Belle's, but dark, almost black.

Canning went out, back to his own room, looked round the door and said:

"He's sleeping, and looks comfortable. Don't worry." What idiotic things one could say at a time like this! He slipped out quickly, and hurried downstairs.

Matthew and Celia were late; they hadn't really given themselves time to get to the quarry and back. Well, they couldn't blame him. He put fried bacon and eggs into the oven, with a low gas, scraped two pieces of toast that he had burned a little, then checked the table to make sure that everything was there.

They arrived at ten past eight, flushed, bright-eyed, breathless.

"I'm so sorry," Celia burst out, "we misjudged it, now we'll have to rush breakfast." She glanced round. "Where's Mother?"

"She has a bad headache," Canning said glibly, "I've given her a cup of tea and some aspirins, and I hope she'll sleep it off. Breakfast's ready in the oven."

Celia went across, tossing her coat over a chair back. Matthew watched her; he could never keep his eyes off her for long.

"What a shame! Can I do anything?"

"Eat your breakfast and get off to work." Canning turned to Matthew. "Matthew, there was—"

"How's Bob?" Celia asked, carrying the dish to the table. She seemed intent on the food, but her question had a studied casualness.

"He had an accident, and cut his face—it rather upset your mother."

"Oh, lord! Is it bad?"

"I don't think so. We'll have the doctor along to look at him. He's asleep now. Matthew—"

"I'm sorry to hear about Bob," Matthew said, and managed to look as if he meant it. Officially he knew nothing about Bob's reputation; quite possibly, however, he knew everything that Celia knew, and that was a great deal. "Sure there's nothing I can do?"

"Quite sure, thanks."

"We'll be late, Matt," Celia said. She was already eating her breakfast. "Dad, you must be famished, do start."

Matthew was also sitting down.

"I will, but I'd like to get a word in first. Matthew, a friend of yours named Jerry telephoned, and said that he wanted you to ring him back. It's urgent."

Matthew paused, with bacon on the end of his fork.

"*Jerry?* Early in the morning!"

"So you call this early, darling," Celia gibed.

Matthew pushed his chair back.

"It's the midnight hours for Jerry, he's a late bird. As if you didn't know! I'll have to see what it's about." He hurried out, and Celia looked at his plate exasperatedly.

"I don't suppose it's worth putting it in the oven to keep warm," she said. "But you needn't let yours spoil, Dad. You can still fry an egg! Did Jerry say what it was about?"

"Not a word."

"Funny," Celia said. "He's a friend of Matt's. You'd hate him!"

"Really?" Canning was mildly sardonic.

"Dance-band leader," Celia said. "Da-da-da and honky-tonk, swing and blues and all that kind of decadent nonsense!" Her eyes were shining. "He's divine!"

"So that's where you get to when you're out until one o'clock in the morning."

"Only once now and again," Celia said defensively, and grimaced at him. "For months I've expected to be told that young girls should be home and in bed long before one. I think this is the time to confide in you. Matthew is of the opinion that you spoil me."

"So the young man has a sense of perception," said Canning dryly. "He's brighter than I'd hoped."

"Don't you say a word against Matt," Celia ordered. "Don't say half a word, he's a dream come true." She pushed her plate aside and laughed. "I get that cosy, comfortable, *snug* feeling when I'm with him, as if I haven't a care in the world."

"Have you?"

She grimaced at him again.

"You know what I mean. And as if I never will have, too. You've never said much about him, Dad. You like him, don't you?"

"Yes. Would it make much difference if I didn't?"

"Not much," Celia admitted seriously, "but it would rather take the gilt off." Abruptly, she went on: "What does Mother really think about him? Or doesn't she tell you?"

"I can't say we talk about him much, but the fact that she's happy to have him here is a pretty good indication, isn't it?"

"Oh, no," said Celia scornfully. Her gaze was both shrewd and penetrating, as if she were trying to dig into his thoughts. "You know better than that, surely. It was a convenient way of scraping together a few pounds a week for Bob. Dad, what's Bob been up to?"

"What on earth are you talking about?"

"He wouldn't come home at five o'clock in the morning, or whenever it was, unless something serious was the matter." Celia had reached for the marmalade. "I suppose he's welched again, and was beaten up." She wasn't callous; just matter-of-fact. "Can't you do *anything* about Bob?"

Canning made himself say gruffly: "You're being embarrassingly frank this morning, aren't you?"

"I suppose I am," Celia said, very soberly. "It isn't often we have five minutes alone, and when we do I'm usually not in the mood. There are times when I could strangle Bob and slap Mother for the way they both—" she broke off, abruptly, jumped up and rounded the table. "Dad I'm sorry, I'm really sorry."

Her hands were on his shoulders. He covered one with his, but didn't look up. Now he knew that Celia wasn't fooled, that she had deceived him with the wisdom of her twenty-two years. He felt choked, was glad that she didn't say more, just turned away.

She picked up her coat.

"Jerry must be crazy, keeping him on the telephone so long," she said tartly. "His breakfast's just a congealed mess." She strode towards the door, but it opened before she reached it. "Matt, if you don't want to be famished all the morn—"

She broke off, startled.

Canning saw a different Matthew. His colour was gone, the amiable look with it; he seemed shocked, and stared with peculiar intentness at Celia for several seconds. She didn't speak. Celia had never been one to talk too much, but now she waited as if in fear. The scene reminded Canning vividly of what had happened when Bob had come back.

Matthew rubbed his forehead, slowly.

"Sorry, sweet. I've had a hell of a shock. So will you have." He went nearer, but didn't touch her. He seemed oblivious of Canning, in whom tension had almost reached screaming point. "That was Jerry. A shocking thing happened last night. Peter was—" he boggled at a word, and still Celia waited, watching him intently, standing very erect. "Oh, hell! Murdered."

Celia echoed in a flat voice: "Peter, murdered."

"Yes. He went home early last night. Had a touch of malaria, Jerry sent him packing and managed with only one sax. No one's sure what happened, but he was found dead in his house. It looks as if he interrupted a burglar, there was a lot of money about on the floor, Jerry says." Matthew talked as if he were shocked beyond coherence. "Peter, of all people." He rubbed his forehead again. "Jerry wants me to be around when his people get back." He put a hand on

Celia's shoulder. "Can you leave at once? Then I can drop you as usual."

"Of course." Celia moved to the door. "Give me two minutes," She hurried out, and Matthew glanced at Canning, who sat as if frozen on his chair.

"My oldest friend. Peter Dale. Good God, it's unbelievable!" Matthew did not seem to notice that Canning was as shocked as he. How could he know that the dark shadow of horror showed in the older man's eyes?" I'd like to get my hands on the swine who did it." He rubbed his forehead again. "Crazy way to talk, isn't it?" He made an obvious effort to pull himself together. "*Murder*."

He began to press his hand against his forehead, as if the burden were unbearable.

Canning couldn't speak.

5

HESITATION

CELIA was gone longer than two minutes, and Matthew stood up and began to fidget. Canning made himself say something. Even though Matthew noticed nothing odd now, he might recall it later on.

"You ought to have something to eat, Matthew. Have some toast and marmalade. I'll pour you out a cup of tea."

"Thanks, I'm not hungry." Matthew still pressed his hand against his head, but he forced a smile. "I'll get over this of course. As I said, Peter was my closest friend. School, everything. It's like losing a brother."

Canning poured out the tea.

"Drink this, and don't be a fool. You'll be hungry by the time you get to Minchester."

Matthew said: "Perhaps you're right." He took the tea and a piece of toast. Celia was still upstairs, she must have been gone for five minutes. "I suppose two minutes always means ten with women." It did with Belle but it didn't with Celia, and he should know that; in fact, he did, words meant nothing. He put marmalade on the toast, forgetting to butter it, half finished his tea, then jumped up. "Here she comes!" He was at the door when Celia appeared again, her hair still falling to her shoulders in a lovely cascade.

"I'm sorry, darling, I couldn't find my lipstick *and* I laddered a stocking." She put a hand on Matthew's arm. "Good-bye, Dad. I hope Mother's soon better."

"She'll be all right."

"Look after yourself! I'll be back about six." She blew him a kiss; that was unusual, they were not a kissing family.

"Good-bye, sir."

Canning managed to sound normal, if a little gruff.

"Good-bye, Matt. I wish I could help."

Matthew gave a taut smile, and raised a hand. They went along the hall passage towards the front door. Usually it was bolted, but Canning hadn't shot the bolts after letting Bob in. The door closed on them quietly, and from that moment there was no sound. Matthew garaged his car at the corner of the road, because Canning's own little Morris filled the garage here.

Canning sat in the silence of the shiny kitchen, with his own empty plate in front of him, Matthew's breakfast congealed on another; the egg had hardened, the bacon was cold and unappetizing. Canning couldn't make himself move. He had no doubt that the murdered man was the one Bob had 'knocked out'. He did not even try to persuade himself that there could have been a coincidence. There was no room for logic in his mind.

It had come to murder.

For years he had known that he wasn't keeping a tight enough rein, that he should defy Belle. He hadn't; he had failed Bob in simple parental duty, and his failure had led to this.

Soon, he began to feel calmer, not particularly emotional. There was a sense of unreality about it all—a dream-like remoteness. He did not blame himself, or the boy, or Belle. The thing had happened and he had to decide what to do; he must be detached about it; objective, anyhow. He lit a cigarette, and the match sounded loud as it scraped on the side of the box.

His son was a murderer, and in this house, and a decision had to be made quickly. Canning knew exactly what he should do. He should pick up the receiver and find out where the murder had been committed; that would easy enough, he was a crony of the editor of the *Minchester Gazette*. Then he should wake Bob, and confirm that he had burgled the same house; make sure that it was the same crime. Finally, he should call the police.

In twenty minutes it would be all over, and Belle need not know what he was doing until the police arrived.

Canning sat where he was, drawing hard at the cigarette. It was one thing to decide to be objective and detached, another to carry out the decision. There was Belle to consider as well as Bob. And himself.

He could say that he felt no pity for Bob, but that wasn't true. It would be easy to be angry, bitter, but—this was his own son. That made it so difficult to be truly objective. Should he be? Could any father? If he handed Bob over to the police, it would be a form of betrayal. This wasn't simply burglary, not even robbery with violence. This was murder and for it his son would be hanged. So if he did what he should, he would be sending Bob to the gallows.

The hope that he was wrong, that Bob's burglary had nothing to do with the murder, crept into his mind.

It faded; he felt a strange, fatalistic certainty.

If anything would drive Belle mad, this would. No matter what he felt towards her, he had to try to help. Against the sudden assault of the shock, she had already shown signs of changing; perhaps a great shock would—

No nonsense! If he handed Bob over to the police he might be taking a risk with Belle's sanity, but that wasn't the real burden of his thoughts. Even if Belle got over the shock, it would be the end of their life together. He had contemplated leaving her often enough, and knew quite well that Celia had really kept him here; but there had always been the shadow of his love, a shadow which at times seemed to have substance, which might become real again. He had never given up hope completely; never reached the stage of thinking that nothing could mend their lives together.

To leave here in this moment of crisis was unthinkable.

Canning went out into the back garden and caught sight of his neighbour's car through the trees. Most men could get out during the day; his work kept him at home a great deal. At least, it was less expensive to work at home, he needed only the small study next to Bob's bedroom. A study, a typewriter and some paper, and pages of carefully compiled notes made during researches at the library in Minchester, and sometimes at the British Museum. He was a freelance journalist who specialized in out-of-the-way articles which sold to national newspapers and magazines as well as obscure little journals. He also did a great deal of translating from French, German and Dutch, into English. He enjoyed the research and liked the people that his business enabled him to meet. He was on the fringe of literature, and if his work was not pretentious, at least it was sound.

It made him his own master, too.

He must go and get dressed, which would mean disturbing Belle.

He passed the telephone. Randall, editor of the *Gazette*, probably wasn't at his office yet.

Canning opened his bedroom door silently, and peered round. Belle lay with her back towards him, and he thought that she was asleep. He crossed the room, took his clothes off a chair, and his collar and tie, loose change and wallet from the dressing-table, and went out. Belle hadn't stirred.

He dressed in the bathroom. It was after nine before he went downstairs. He passed the telephone again.

They had a charwoman three times a week, but this wasn't one of her mornings. He began the washing-up. By the time he finished, it was a quarter to ten. He had no excuse now, Randall would be at his desk, all agog about the local murder. Once he lifted the telephone he would set the grim business in motion.

The telephone bell rang.

Canning felt his heart turn over, and stood quite still, while the bell went on ringing. Then he hurried forward and snatched the receiver up.

"Hallo—Canning here."

"I've a London call for you," the operator said.

London.

Canning leaned against the wall, sweating; this was a business call, there was no need for fear.

"Mr. Canning?" a different girl asked.

"Yes."

"Mr. Grayson would like to speak to you, hold on, please."

Grayson was the editor of a popular weekly magazine who often commissioned an article and always wanted it in a desperate hurry. As he waited, Canning watched the landing; no one stirred up there. Then Grayson came on the line, an urgent man. Had Canning seen the morning papers? No. There had been an air cash in the Sahara; forty passengers had survived and were stranded two hundred miles from a town. How quickly could Canning write an article on the nomad tribes in the vicinity? This was one of Grayson's easiest requests. Yes, Canning could have twenty-four hours; that would enable Grayson to be up-to-the-minute in a weekly magazine, for publication would probably coincide with the rescue.

"Fine, thanks," Grayson said briskly. "Good-bye, old chap."

As Canning moved away from the telephone, pictures of the nomad Arab tribes of the Sahara were coming into his mind. This was the old, tried and trusted refuge; work. He was tempted to go up to the loft, where he kept his files of out-of-the-way information.

There was no sound at either bedroom door.

He ought to telephone Randall—

He went into his study, a small room with books on open shelves which stretched to the ceiling; a library ladder stood in front of one row, and a loft ladder worked by a pulley was drawn up to the ceiling. His desk was placed by the window. He sat down in his swivel chair, in front of his tidy desk.

He ought to telephone Randall, and find out for certain whether—

What difference would a few hours make?

He jumped up, strode across to the loft ladder, lowered it and hurried up. He went to his files on 'North Africa—People'. His mind wasn't really free but at moments the subject held his interest.

He stayed for half an hour, then went down to the study again. All was silent. He looked into Bob's room; the boy was still sleeping. He would not give himself time to study the relaxed features, the way the dark lashes lay upon the sallow cheeks.

In the study, Canning put the notes into proper order; it was now simply a question of writing the article.

If Bob's shoulder hadn't improved, they would have to send for the doctor. Would the doctor immediately connect the knife wound in Bob's cheek with the murder? Why should he? The victim had fallen and struck his head against a chair. *Was* that truly murder? Or manslaughter? He had let the word murder become an obsession.

It was peaceful this morning; no humming of the vacuum cleaner, no movements of Belle or the daily woman about the house. The article was practically writing itself. Good Lord! He hadn't been to the porch for the morning paper or for the letters; both postman and newspaper boy always arrived late. He didn't go downstairs. If he could finish the article before Bob or Belle stirred, he would have that off his mind. Grayson was a valuable customer, and must be kept happy.

How was Bob's shoulder? How was Belle? *Was* it possible that two different men had been hurt? Was Bob's victim dead—or alive?

He stopped typing. Another hour or so's work, and it would be finished. It was nearly twelve o'clock.

His door opened.

"I thought I heard the typewriter," Belle said.

She hadn't dressed or washed, her hair was untidy and flattened down against her head. She pushed the door to and went across to his leather armchair and sat on the arm.

"How are you, dear?" Canning forced himself to ask.

"My headache's better." Belle forced a smile; she seemed worn out. Perhaps it would have been truer to say that she looked as if all vitality had been drained out of her. "Bob's still asleep."

"I keep looking in."

"You—you haven't done anything, George, have you?"

"Not yet."

"But you still think you should. I know, in some ways you're right. I've been lying awake, thinking. If it were anyone else's son, I'd think it wrong to try to hide anything. When it's your own son, its different." Her voice was flat and monotonous. That was the shock, of course; it also explained her odd, unusual manner. What would happen if she knew the whole truth? She would have to know, soon.

But what *was* the truth?

"George," Belle said, very slowly, huskily, "I keep thinking about that man, the man Bob knocked out. I suppose he's all right. If—if he saw Bob—"

This was the moment to tell her. It was on the tip of Canning's tongue, but he held the words back. He wasn't quite sure of the truth; until he was he must not give her a new, shattering blow.

"Will you go to Minchester and find out?" Belle asked.

6

MINCHESTER

Canning drove through the crowded streets of the cathedral town at a snail's pace. It was Wednesday, Market Day and it was astonishing that people from the villages still ambled across the road as if they had nothing more to fear than an occasional carriage or a horse. The sun shone warmly from a cloudless sky and showed the old buildings in sharp relief. Gabled roofs, sinking red tiles covered with lichen, white walls strengthened by great oak beams, made Minchester more attractive than most country towns. The wide High Street was filled, near the sixteenth-century Town Hall, with the market stalls. Parking was a problem on Market Day, and Canning drove along a narrow street to the back of the *Gazette* building. There was a private parking plot which Randall made free to his friends.

Canning put the Morris next to Randall's big Austin, and went in at the back door, through the printing room. Thudding machines were devouring newsprint; there was the sharp smell of printing ink. Two or three of the workmen recognized and acknowledged Canning as he went through a narrow door into a small room where four men were busy at monotype machines, working as if mechanically. Another door led to the advertising office and stairs to Randall's office and the reporters' room.

Canning had left home twenty minutes after Belle had asked him to come here. It had been easy to persuade himself that it would be much better to drop in casually and let Randall bring up the subject of the murder; to ask about it by telephone might imply that he had some special interest. He had driven very carefully, still trying to get his thoughts straight, still quite certain about what he ought to do if Bob had killed the man.

Standing outside the closed door of Randall's room,

marked with a large PRIVATE and a smaller *Keep Out*, he realized what had happened. If the murder had been committed at a different house, he would allow himself to be persuaded into keeping quiet about Bob's burglary. So much for his boasted principles!

He tapped and went in.

Randall looked up from his big littered desk, obviously annoyed. Another man, opposite him, glanced round. Canning stood there, startled, even shocked; the other man was Banfield, the Minchester Superintendent of Police.

Randall's look of annoyance quickly faded.

"Hallo, George. Mind waiting for five minutes? We won't be longer, will we, Ted?"

"Less, I hope," Banfield said. " 'Morning, George."

" 'Morning, Of course I'll wait." Canning was glad to close the door. Usually he would have gone into the reporters' room and had a word with whoever was inside; this time he went downstairs. His nerves were in a bad way. He knew Banfield fairly well, as he knew most of the public men in Minchester. It wasn't the first time he had gone into Randall's office and found the policeman there, either; but he felt as if the two were in a conspiracy against him. Had they noticed anything? He lit a cigarette and went into the High Street, where half a dozen people were gathered about the photographs displayed in the *Gazette* window. Banfield's car stood outside. Men calling their wares in the market threw their voices until they travelled up and down the street. Every stall seemed to have a crowd round it. Woolworth's, opposite the *Gazette*, looked as if it were jammed tight with people. Three doors away from Woolworth's was a tall Georgian building, now turned into offices. Celia worked on the third floor, Matthew one floor below.

"Why, hallo." Matthew's voice sounded in his ear. Canning started as he turned round. "I didn't know you were coming in this morning."

"I wasn't—had to look up something in the library," Canning said. Matthew seemed much more his normal self; it was only when Canning looked closely that he saw signs of strain, and he realized that the smile did not come freely. He had to say something. "How are things going?"

"It's still grim," Matthew said. "Devil of a business."

"It must be."

"How's Mrs. Canning?"

"Oh, she's all right now."

"Bob?"

"Still asleep."

"That's good." Matthew spoke quite casually, there seemed no change in his tone when he inquired about Bob. Why should there be? What could possibly make him suspect—

"Ah, here's Jerry," Matthew went on, his tone changing. A plump young man of medium height, wearing a well-fitting grey suit, drew up. His full cheeks were pasty and he had a small mouth. He looked out of sorts. "Hallo, Jerry. You haven't met Celia's father, have you? Mr. Canning, Mr. Jerry Dale."

"Good morning."

"How're you?" Jerry wasn't interested in Canning. "Isn't he here yet?"

"His car's there," Matthew said, and glanced at Banfield's black Wolseley. "He won't be long. We're meeting the Chief of Police here, Superin—but of course you know him, don't you?"

"Yes." Canning was glad that the younger men were on edge, Jerry especially, and taking little notice of him. He wanted to know why Matthew was going to see Banfield; what business was it of his? His own question exasperated him; Jerry was the murdered Peter's brother, the police would need to talk to him—and Matthew was a close friend. Matthew was the kind of friend who would stand by.

Canning didn't need to meet Jerry's eyes, they were turned towards the *Gazette* doors.

"I needn't say that I'm—"

"Ah, here he is!" Jerry broke in on the words, probably without realizing that they were meant for him.

Banfield came out of the *Gazette* building. He was a big, bulky, quick-moving man dressed in brown, with a long chin, a long nose; a big Punch of a man.

"Sorry if I kept you," he said. "Hallo, George, all clear up there now." He opened the door of the car.

Jerry forgot to nod or speak to Canning; Matthew said: "See you later," and got into Banfield's car. Canning didn't wait to see it drive off, but went in the building and hurried up the stairs. If he hadn't hurried, he would have funked the interview; the last thing he really wanted was a talk with Randall. But that was only because Randall had been talking to the Superintendent, and was nonsense. He must steady his nerves.

He tapped and waited.

"Come in."

Canning went in, and Randall grinned.

"Getting polite, aren't you?"

"I learned my lesson," Canning said, and managed to smile. He sat down heavily. "How are you, Jim?"

"Usual rude health, and with too much work to do," Randall said, "but always time for a chat with you. Like a cup of tea? I'm just going to have one, but Ted wouldn't stay." Randall had tea at all hours, day and night. "Ted is having a Roman holiday."

"Really?"

"It's only his third murder in seventeen years," Randall said, and chuckled. "You can imagine, he'll spread himself!" He flicked down the key of a loud-speaker telephone. "Send in tea for two, please," then flicked it off. His good humour faded. Randall was a rubicund man, fresh-faced, as shrewd as men came, although strangers often saw only the genial fellow who overdid the jocularity. "I hope he gets the swine soon. You've heard about it, of course."

"Yes."

"It would have shaken up the town anyway," Randall said. "Being Peter Dale it will rock the place. One of the most popular of the younger set, and a nice chap. I prefer him to his brother, although Jerry is as clever in his way. How much *do* you know?"

"His friend Grant is living with us."

"Oh, yes, of course. Banfield's going to meet Matt Grant and Jerry now. Matt's been a friend of the family for so long he's almost one of them. The mother and father were on holiday in Cornwall, they're due back this afternoon. I didn't know them, kept themselves to themselves a lot." Randall sniffed. "But it will be a hell of a blow. I gather that Jerry nearly folded up, and Matt Grant is keeping him going."

"That doesn't surprise me." Canning was hungry for more details, but didn't know how to ask the leading questions. "I gather Jerry and his brother were in a dance band."

"*The* band in the district, with radio and television contracts, too. I'm expecting a Fleet Street invasion at any minute."

"Where was it?" Canning asked, and realized sickeningly that he should have asked: "Just what happened?"

"Marlborough Road—one of the big houses near the Park. The irony is that Peter Dale wouldn't normally have gone home when he did. He suffers from bouts of malaria and was caught short last night. Jerry sent him home. It only happens once or twice a year. The house was empty, with the parents away and the servants too. Between you and me, I think Banfield has a pretty shrewd idea who did it."

Canning just said: "Oh," and felt as if he were being suffocated.

"There are two servants, man and wife. Polish fellow, Scots girl, a youngish couple." Randall was full of the story. "The Dale boys have always been careless about money and they both follow form and back their fancy. They pulled off a double on Saturday and came back with notes spilling out of their pockets. Most people would have banked them first thing on Monday morning, but Jerry was planning another day at the races to-day, and kept it in the house. The servants were there when he came home on Saturday, didn't go off until next day. So they knew all about it. Banfield's pretty canny and wouldn't say so, but his eyes are on the Pole—gardener and odd-job man."

Canning said gruffly: "Has he any evidence?"

"I don't know, yet. These Poles are always a bit ready with a knife—all right, all right, I withdraw, you hate generalizations!" Randall grinned. "Let's say that some of the Poles who've settled over here have been a bit too handy with a knife. Satisfy you?"

"That's better." Canning still felt suffocated. "So it was a knife."

"Stabbed through the throat," Randall said shortly.

Stabbed; so the victim hadn't cracked his skull in the fall; if this were the man who had surprised Bob, then Bob knew that he was dead.

"He'd been knocked about, too, had a nasty wound at the back of his head and several cuts about the hands," Randall went on. "The killer seems to have gone into a panic. He left two hundred pounds or so on the floor. Apparently Peter caught him as he was getting away." Randall glanced up at a tap at the door; called come in, and got up to take a tray from a pretty, fluffy-haired girl who brought in the tea. "I thought you'd forgotten all about us, Queenie." The girl gave a quick, embarrassed smile, and hurried out. Randall grinned. "Nice to have one who's shy, for a change, bold as brass most of them, these days. How's Celia?"

"As fit as ever."

"Good. You don't take sugar, do you? Well, what's brought you in, George? It wasn't to talk about sordid things like murder, I know!"

"I had to look in at the library and felt like a cup of tea," Canning said. He didn't want to change the subject, there were still so many questions. He couldn't keep his mind on anything else, but it didn't greatly matter, Randall liked to hear himself talking.

Canning's thoughts roamed. Would Banfield suspect the Polish gardener without a good reason? According to Bob, he had knocked his man out—or rather the man had been knocked out by the chair—and fled. It was the other man who had held a knife. The Pole might have come in afterwards. That wasn't convincing, it was just something to seize on as a reason for hope.

"Well, George, I've a lot to do," Randall said bluffly. "Why not have lunch with me if you're staying in town?" He glanced at his watch. "Good Lord, it's getting on for one, I've never known a morning fly like it. I can't leave for at least an hour. What about—"

"I have to get back, I'm on a rush job for Grayson."

"So he's at it again." Randall stood up. They didn't shake hands, just grinned at each other.

Canning went out and slowly down the stairs. There was nothing else he could usefully do here, although he hated the thought of going back and telling Belle about this; Bob, too, for that matter. What grounds were there for hoping that Bob hadn't killed the man? If he had, it meant that he had lied about the knife; no, about leaving the man unconscious and not knowing how badly hurt he was. Bob could be expected to try to lie his way out of anything. It was possible that Peter Dale had used a knife; finding a burglar in the house he would need some kind of weapon. If they'd struggled for the weapon, the fatal wound might have been made almost accidentally; Bob had that wound in his cheek, it certainly wasn't self-inflicted.

Canning found himself thinking less and less about the plight of the suspect gardener. It was stretching coincidence too far to believe that two men had gone to burgle the house at about the same time. Banfield was on the wrong track. That not only gave Bob breathing space, but gave Canning time to force the truth out of Bob.

If Belle's present mood lasted, she would probably help to persuade Bob to talk. Belle rational about the boy would be unique. She never had been; it was as if Bob's birth had implanted viciousness in her.

Canning sat at the wheel of his car, hearing the noise of the printing machines in the *Gazette* works, when that thought passed through his mind.

"Don't be a damned fool," he muttered.

But the thought wouldn't fade.

Belle had shown qualities of viciousness and deceit which made it possible that the boy had inherited his bad traits from her. There was plenty in this hereditary business. But now Canning had to deal with effects, not causes; the first thing was to prise the truth out of Bob.

The day was perfect. The countryside had never seemed lovelier, the hedges were just begining to sprout new growth, the road out to Lingham was narrow and winding, passing through two villages with thatched cottages and an old-world charm at which some sneered but which Canning liked. It was driving through here that he usually felt the touch of peace which the countryside gave him; along this road, going back to Belle and to an atmosphere he hated, that he let his thoughts wander. Often, they were about leaving her; he wished bitterly that he had taken the plunge, years ago.

He turned the corner by the garage where Matthew kept his car, and drove up the hilly road towards his house, *Hillview;* the previous owner had christened it. The car jolted over the rough surface. Two or three neighbours were in their gardens—a lot of retired people lived here. Two waved.

There was a car outside *Hillview*, but room for Canning to drive between the gates. He realized that the car was a black Wolseley.

He had a vivid picture of Banfield opening the doors of his car. The feeling of suffocation came over him. He jammed on the brakes, then put the gear into neutral.

Could the police have come here?

The front door opened, and Belle waved from the porch. She vanished almost at once. If the police were questioning Bob, would she have seemed so calm?

Canning left the car outside the garage and hurried to the back door. Belle was going upstairs when he reached the hall. He could hardly get the words out.

"Who is it?"

"Dr. Hall," Belle explained. "Bob's shoulder was so swollen I had to send for him, in case anything was broken. He's with him now."

7

THE TRUTH?

DR. HALL practised in Lingham, wasn't a Minchester man. Could there be any reason why he should connect Bob's injuries with the murder? Canning persuaded himself that there was none.

He went into the kitchen.

A cold lunch was on the kitchen table; so Belle was keeping her head. The calmness of her voice when she had told him about the doctor promised well. Yet it wasn't the Belle he knew; he couldn't quite understand the difference, but there was one.

Was she playing a part?

Canning went into the dining-room, and helped himself to a whisky and soda, listening to the faint sounds overhead. Soon he heard voices, and a man's footsteps. Hall was elderly, stout, and heavy-footed.

"Please yourself, Mrs. Canning, please yourself." He sounded his bluff self. "You'd be sure with an X-Ray, that's all. I don't think it's more than a bad bruise. Cold compresses three times a day, and the swelling should be down before long. I'll look in again the day after to-morrow, unless you send for me."

"Thank you, doctor."

"How's your husband?"

"Very well," Belle said.

"That's good, that's good."

Dr. Hall went out of the front door. Belle closed it and came along to the dining-room. She wore a clinging woollen dress, of wine red, which emphasized her figure—it was the figure of a young woman, almost as provocative as Celia's.

She'd made up, too. She wasn't the aloof, cold woman of so many yesterdays, and her voice was quiet, with no hint of stridency.

"Hallo George. He doesn't think it's more than a bruise."

"No, I heard."

"We've put on a compress. He dressed that cut, too, says it's nothing to worry about," Belle went on. "Bob says his face is stiff, that's all. He's up." Her eyes were questioning. "He'll be down in a moment."

"Good."

A sharper note came into Belle's voice; a note of urgency, perhaps of fear.

"Well, what did you find out?"

Canning said: "My dear, I don't think there's anything to be gained by telling you half a story. I'm afraid it's going to be a shock." He was surprised that his voice was so gentle, that he was so distressed because he had to hurt her. "It couldn't be much worse."

Belle put a hand on the dining-room table, and leaned heavily on it. There was no colour in her face, except in her tormented eyes.

"What—what is it?"

"The man is dead."

She didn't speak; but for the table, she might have fallen. Canning went forward, and slid his arm round her waist. He could have been holding a statue, she was so stiff. He made her move to a chair, and helped her to sit down; she kept silent, staring at the french windows which opened on to a narrow lawn with flower beds on either side. He poured out a finger of brandy, and held it to her lips.

"Drink this."

She moved her head back and looked at the glass, then opened her mouth obediently, putting one hand up to steady the glass. She hardly seemed to realize that she was drinking.

Above their heads, Bob was moving about.

"I'll have to talk to Bob," Canning said.

That did not make her speak.

"Belle, I wish to God it was anything but this!"

She did not even turn her head to look at him. He stared at the mask of her face, and wondered if her mind were working at all, or whether she was numbed in mind as well as body. Footsteps sounded on the stairs. He hurried to the door, reaching it as Bob was on the last step. Bob stopped, abruptly.

"Hal—hallo, Dad." Obviously he was nervous about his reception. There was no defiance in him; his fine dark eyes reflected his own fear.

In that moment, Canning thought: "He knows." But he didn't think much about Bob just then; only about Belle. "Bob, your mother's not well, and this is a great strain for her. I'll come and see you in a moment."

"Okay. I—I'm sorry."

Canning nodded, went in and closed the door. Belle hadn't moved. He went in front of her, and she looked up at him, her eyes glassy.

"Listen, Belle, I must talk to Bob and find out what really happened. Will you be all right here for ten minutes?"

She opened her lips; it was like looking at a ventriloquist's doll.

"I suppose so."

"Is there anything I can get you?"

"No."

"I won't be long," Canning said, "and I'll be as—as gentle as I can." He went out, casting a look back at his wife's unmoving figure, then saw Bob in the kitchen. He went in briskly thankful that he felt little emotion; it was as if feeling had been drained out of him, except for Belle; and that was creeping back.

Bob was making a ham sandwich, clumsily. The bread was cut and the ham sliced. He stopped, gulped and smiled uneasily.

"Afraid I'm starving."

"I expect you are. Get on with it." Canning lit a cigarette.

The new dressing on Bob's face was larger, stretching from

the side of his nose right over the left cheek. He held his left shoulder and side very stiffly, and his arm was in a sling, a dark coat slung over his shoulder. He kept glancing uneasily at Canning.

"Dad, I—I really am awfully sorry. I know it was a hell of a thing to do. I promise you that I'll never—" he gulped again, and couldn't finish. "I'm sorry," he added lamely. The sandwich was made but he didn't begin to eat it. "I really am."

"Bob, I want to know exactly what happened last night, after the man surprised you."

"I've told you."

"Everything?"

"Yes."

It wasn't true, Canning thought wearily. He would have to use pressure, and didn't know how he was going to do that without revealing the truth. Once that was out, Bob would probably lie himself sick.

"Eat your sandwich," Canning said abruptly. Then: "You know what I think about the way you've gone on, but this is something quite different. I don't propose to rake up the past. But you must understand that the consequences of this can be very grave indeed. I want to help you. The only way I can help you is by hearing the whole truth, with nothing at all left out. Do you understand that?"

"Yes." Bob was eating. "I've told you everything."

"Let's see if I remember it properly. The man was approaching you with a knife in his hand, you hit him, he cut your cheek with the knife, then you knocked him down and he struck his head on the back of a chair. You left him unconscious."

"Yes, and that's the lot. I—I know I ought to have made sure he was all right, but I couldn't get out of the house quick enough."

"Was it the Dales' house, in Marlborough Road?"

"Good Lord, how did you know that?" Bob gaped.

"I've been trying to find out what's known in Minchester," Canning said carefully. He had to be very cautious indeed.

Now he knew that this was the same crime, beyond any shadow of doubt. He made himself go on: "Did you get the knife away from the man?"

"It fell."

"Did you pick it up?"

"No. I wouldn't touch the damned thing. I—I tell you I was scared out of my wits. I was all the time, and when I saw that chap— "

"Do you know who he was?"

"No. I'd got a torch, but it wasn't on. I wouldn't have seen him, but a car passed just as I was going to the hall, and it shone into the room. That was the first time I knew anyone was there. If it hadn't been for that car, I would have walked right into him."

"And you didn't touch the knife."

"Listen, Dad, I *am* telling you the truth," Bob said.

The trouble was that he had often sworn that a lie was the truth. He looked earnest enough, and the furtive, almost sly look that was sometimes in his eyes wasn't there; but he would know that he dared not fail to convince. Probably he thought that the only thing at stake was his freedom from a charge of burglary, but that would be vital enough for him.

"All right," Canning said. "Now tell me how it was that you knew there would be money in the house, and why you thought that no one else would be there?"

"Well—" Bob put his right hand to his pocket, pulled out a silver cigarette case and opened it awkwardly; it was empty. "Would you give me a fag?"

Canning gave him one, and lit it.

"Thanks a lot, Dad. Well, I was over at Garnett on Saturday. You know, the racecourse. I saw the Dales collect a big pile of notes from a bookie." He managed not to evade Canning's eyes. "I know you hate me betting, but I can't help it, I *have* to! I'd lost every penny I had. I still felt mad at you, and didn't want to come home, but I had to get some money. Then some of the chaps and I started talking, and one of them said that the Dales' old folk had gone away. Jerry leads a dance band, and—"

"I know that."

"Oh. Well, apparently Jerry and his brother, that's Peter, were going to have their meals at a hotel. One of the chaps I was with is receptionist at the *George & Dragon*, so he knew the house would be empty most of the time. I knew Jerry and Peter wouldn't be home until about two-thirty, there was a big dance that night, they were playing until two. So I thought it would be easy. The chaps were talking about Jerry keeping a lot of money at the house." Bob's gaze fell at last. "As a matter of fact I'd seen where he kept it, some of it, anyway."

"So, you'd been to the house before."

"Yes, only once. He gave me an audition, when I was playing the trumpet. No go, really, but he said I might come on if I practised enough. While I was there he went into another room and I saw him through a crack in the door. There was kind of secret door at the back of a sideboard, and he just pressed a button and it opened. He took out a great wad of pound notes and fivers." Bob gulped again. "I *am* telling you everything, Dad, but now I can see what a swine I was."

If he had escaped with the money, he would probably have thought himself a genius.

Canning didn't comment. He felt on edge, because this was taking longer than he had thought, and Belle might still be sitting in the dining-room, stiff, numbed, frightened.

"All right," Canning said. "I suppose you know that the police will almost certainly discover that it was you."

Bob moved forward a step. His voice squeaked. "I don't see how they can!" That had caught him on the raw, the fear was back. "That—that's if you don't tell them. I—I wore gloves, I didn't leave any fingerprints or anything."

Canning felt like sneering: "Quite the professional." The impulse faded.

"The police don't miss much, Bob. I shouldn't be too sure about what they'll find. Now, have I your word for it that you didn't touch that knife?"

"It—it touched *me*. I—I had to fight to stop him using it; he'd have killed me."

"Did you take it from him?"

"I—"

"*Did you?*"

"I knocked it out of his hand," Bob muttered. "That's all."

"Did you pick it up?"

"I *did* just pick it up," Bob admitted. His gaze shifted again. "I was wearing the gloves, I didn't see that it mattered. As a matter of fact I trod on it, and just picked it up without thinking, you know how you do."

Canning could hardly force words out:

"That was when he was unconscious?"

"Why, of course."

"And you stopped to pick up the knife and look at it, although you didn't trouble to shine your torch into his face and see whether he was all right?"

"No. No, I didn't, I—I hardly knew what I was doing. *Can't* you understand?"

"I'm afraid I do understand," Canning said bitterly. He wanted to thrust the boy away from him, anger welled up and killed all pity. It was impossible to distinguish the truth from the lies; once he knew that Peter Dale was dead, Bob would probably tell a totally different story. "I've been into Minchester, as I told you."

Bob licked his lips.

"Yes, did you—did you find anything out?" Panic flared into his eyes, he stretched out his right hand and touched his father's. "You didn't go to the police, did you? They aren't after me?"

"I didn't tell the police anything," Canning said.

"God, you scared me!" Bob drew back, looking as if he would collapse. "Dad, if you—if you help me this time, I swear I won't play the fool again. You'll never have to complain. I'll get a steady job and settle down. You'll be able to trust me." His voice quivered.

Canning didn't speak. Bob came up against the kitchen

table, and leaned on it heavily. A knife fell, and clattered.

"Dad," whispered Bob, "what happened? What did you find out?"

There was a long pause; fear stopped him from going on. His lips began to work; what would cause such dread if he did not know the truth?

"*What did you find out?*"

Canning said very quietly: "The man was Peter Dale. He died. You knew he was dead, didn't you? You kil—"

"No!" screamed Bob.

The cry was of anguish, and horror. It cut Canning's words short; and there was a moment of taut silence.

Then, words exploded from the trembling lips.

"No, it's not true!" Bob's right arm rose and thrust outwards, as if to keep off a physical threat. "I didn't kill him! I didn't know he was dead. Oh, no, he's not dead, that couldn't have happened, it couldn't. No, no, *no*."

"Listen, Bob," Canning said in the same quiet voice, "Peter Dale was found dead by his brother. I don't think it will be possible to save you from the police. If the local police don't get on to you soon, they'll send for Scotland Yard. I think you'll have to make up your mind that you'll be found out. The sensible thing would be for you to go and tell the police everything."

"But he wasn't dead, he couldn't have been, he only knocked his head on a chair!"

"If that's the truth, then tell the police at once."

"But he's dead, they—" Bob couldn't find the words; he mouthed sounds that were only gibberish; the ugly exhibition was far worse than anything that had gone before. Canning felt sure that his son had known all the time that Dale was dead, but would never admit it. He would probably believe that if he said "I didn't" often enough, his word would be accepted.

Words sounded again. "I couldn't tell the police, Dad. I couldn't, you've got to save me."

The door opened, and Belle came in. She was very quiet;

unnatural. She didn't smile, nor did she look with the expected venom at Canning.

"Of course we shall keep you safe," she said. "The police may never find out that it was you. Your father is exaggerating." She actually found a smile for Canning. "Don't upset yourself, Bob. It was a terrible thing to do, but you're our child, you can rely on us absolutely. George, I'd like to talk to you, please. You must be hungry, Bob, have something to eat at once."

She gave the mockery of a smile again, then went out quite sure that Canning would follow her.

Bob watched her until she disappeared. His lips trembled, his body shook. It was fear of the gallows, there was no remorse in him. Perhaps there hadn't been time for that, Canning thought miserably. He watched the boy, and saw him as a stranger; in some ways, he was a stranger. Once the police found him and began their questions, he would condemn himself by his own contradictions, by his lies. There was no chance for him—how could there be? He had handled the knife. Probably he had torn it from Peter Dale's grasp and struck out blindly; there may have been no intent to kill. That was the best anyone could make of it, but it would still be murder. A twenty-year-old boy would have no mercy from the law.

Belle was at the door.

"George, please come," she said.

8

BELLE

Canning left his son crouching by the table, and went into the hall. Belle was walking towards the open front door. On the telephone table were the morning newspaper and several letters; so she had opened the box, had behaved quite rationally since he had left her. The sun came warmly into the porch, and when they went into the garden, it was almost too warm. Belle led the way to one of the lawns and they walked, as they did most days when the weather was fine, along the flower beds. The tulips had opened their heads to the sun, the daffodils were glowing with a glory that would soon fade, and the brightness brought out the soft, deep colours of the wallflowers. This was another refuge, one they had always been able to share; but Canning hardly looked at the flowers.

"I don't want Bob to hear us," Belle said, "there's no sense in making it worse for him than it need be, is there?"

"Belle, I don't want—"

She looked at him with a smile which was almost fond.

"I know how you feel, George, and although you won't believe it, I can understand. I can see now what a burden Bob has been. I can also see that I've been wrong most of the time. We should have worked together, and the fault is mine. You tried, as far as I would let you. And being you, of course, you were tormented because you weren't able to do everything you thought was right. You see, I do understand."

Canning nodded dumbly.

"But whatever happened in the past, we've got to deal with this, haven't we?" Belle went on. "You want to send Bob to the police, or fetch them here. For the last time, I'm going to have my way."

Canning didn't speak.

"I mean it when I say for the last time," Belle said quietly. "I wonder if you can imagine what it feels like to wake up suddenly and find that you've been wrong for years. I hated you last night. I hated you when you said we shouldn't shield Bob. The shock did something to me. And since you've been back from Minchester and we know the worst—" she paused; Canning thought that she was going to touch his arm, but she kept apart from him and looked, now, at the distant trees. "I think it's shocked me into knowing how wrong I was. I keep thinking that if you had had your way, this would probably never have happened. Can you imagine how that hurts? How I blame myself?"

Canning made himself say awkwardly: "You thought you were acting for the best."

"That doesn't make it easier now," she said. "Above everything else I'm trying to be sensible about it. I feel that if I let myself go, I shall go mad. Sitting in the dining-room before you left me, I wanted to rave and scream at you, to curse you."

"Belle, don't—"

"I've nearly finished, George. There's just this last thing I want you to do for me. I don't think it's quite what you expect. Don't go to the police. Don't do anything to bring them here. Let him go to them."

"But he'll never do that!" Canning burst out.

"I'm not so sure," Belle said. "You've already put the idea into his head. Have you ever seen him looking as he did just now? I seemed to be seeing an image of myself. He felt as I've felt. He realized the folly of all he's done. Give him this chance. If we're practical about it, we have to admit that the police will probably find out he was at the house, don't we?"

"I think so."

"Bob will realize that, too. He'll realize that it's better to give himself up. At least, let's give him the chance. No one would blame a father for trying to help his own son. You would never be blamed and you needn't blame yourself. It's really giving him the chance you wanted, isn't it? A kind of—" she paused, searching for words. "A kind of purgatory for him. When he's passed through it, he'll be different. At least he *might* be. Give him a chance to find himself. If he does that, then we can surely stand whatever follows."

Again she hesitated, and they stood facing each other; her eyes were calm, almost serene, as if she knew that she could influence Canning best this way.

"Even if he were to be hanged," she added deliberately.

After a pause, Canning said: "Belle, I don't know what to say. I can hardly think."

"You think too much. I've always thought that, dear. But you can think about this, George, there's no desperate hurry. Try to give him this last chance."

"Belle, you know that he'll have to face up to it eventually, don't you? We can't let him escape. If the police shouldn't trace him—"

"He'll go to them."

"I wish I thought so," Canning said heavily.

"Would you have believed that I would talk like this?"

He gave a twisted smile. "No. Not lately, my dear. Once—"

She took his hand for the first time.

"If I can be shocked into changing, so can Bob. I'll do all I can to help. I'll reason with him—oh, I won't try to persuade him to give himself up, he has to make the decision, himself. I'll just try to make him see your point of view. Try to help so far, George."

"How long do you want?" Canning asked abruptly. "How long do you think it will take? If you're wrong, the longer he's free the safer he will feel."

"Give him a few days. A week." Her hold on Canning's hand was very tight. "If he hasn't told the police at the end of the week, then you'll have to tell them."

After a long silence, he said:

"If I do—I don't know what to say, but even if I should agree, it might do him harm, eventually. If the police get on to him half-way through the week, and he's said nothing, then it will look much worse for him. If he tells them now—"

"I'll take that chance, George," Belle said.

"Give me an hour or two to think it over," Canning asked heavily.

"Of course," she agreed freely. "And I ought to go back to Bob, it wouldn't do to leave him on his own too much. If I were you, I shouldn't talk to him until you've decided." She smiled again. "If you do, you'll start trying to make him promise—just as I'm trying to make you."

"You go and see him," Canning said gruffly.

He watched her walking towards the house, tall, slim, graceful. They had lived here for fifteen years, and in this garden he had never felt about her as he did now. He had yearned, had desired her; but he had never known real hope of understanding. Was this real? Had the shock truly affected her, or had she realized that no ordinary plea would shake him? Was she showing great cunning? He remembered how she had sat like a statue, incapable of movement; what had she really been thinking?

If she had changed, and if he did as she had begged, would that breathe life into their future?

Canning walked aimlessly about the garden. How right was she? He did not really believe that there was any hope that Bob would give himself up. He had a streak of cowardice, and that would keep him back. It was easy to imagine him cringing, begging for mercy.

Other thoughts crept in.

What right had a man to condemn his own son? To send him to trial for murder, and to the gallows?

The decision might not rest with him, Canning calmed himself. Banfield might find the trail here; if he should fail, Scotland Yard would surely succeed. There was Celia, too, and Matthew. The fact that Matthew was spending so much time with Jerry Dale meant that he could be thinking only of the murder. What would happen if he guessed the truth? Or Celia, who was more likely to? A knife wound in the cheek, a man stabbed to death—how could she fail to connect the two?

Was his mind too sensitive? Did his knowledge make him think that others would have some kind of prescience?

The sun burned down, and the wind had dropped; he was too hot. He walked across the lawns towards the trees by the side of the drive, and, in their shade, back to the house. The kitchen was empty. He heard Belle talking quietly in the drawing-room, and wished he could hear what she said. He stood by the door, but only a murmur of her voice came through.

He was dazzled by a burning hope; that he could free himself and Belle from the thraldom of those twenty wasted bitter years. Why had she ever changed? A futile question: his thoughts were chaotic. Why *had* she changed? They had known two years of happiness, before Celia had been born; for two years after that he had noticed no great change; then Bob, and Belle had become a stranger.

Kingley, a Minchester doctor whom Canning knew well, had once talked to him, Randall and half a dozen others about cases where childbirth had affected a woman's mental balance. There were fierce arguments in the medical profession, Kingley had said, about whether the trouble had been latent all the time and simply brought to the surface by the ordeal of childbearing; or whether some new factor was introduced. Kingley supported the latent trouble theory. Canning had listened intently, but gained little satisfaction.

There wasn't much point in thinking about Kingley and his theores now. He had to make up his mind.

In fact, he had already made up his mind. He would agree.

He went up to his study, sat in the armchair and smoked, found fresh thought seeping into his mind, started by the sight of the unfinished page in the typewriter. The article could be finished in an hour; he could still catch the post. He hadn't to think about it, only to elaborate the facts he had already assembled. He went to the desk. His fingers were slow and fumbling on the typewriter at first; gradually, he found his touch. A kind of peace, almost the only kind he knew, stole over him.

He had finished and was reading the article through when Belle opened the door.

"I've brought you some tea, George."

"Oh. Fine. Thanks." More often than not she would thrust open the door and say: "Tea." and go out again. There was only one cup on the tray; but the newspaper and the post were with it.

"I'm glad you can work," she said.

"It's an urgent job, for the *Roamer*."

"Good. If you're going to catch the post I'll walk down

with you. Bob's much quieter." She didn't stay to talk; it was as if she were determined not to harass or hurry him. He went to the easy chair and poured out tea, then opened the letters. Two trifling commissions, a cheque, two bills; nothing of much importance. He drank tea and glanced through the newspaper, reading the story of the air crash for the first time. Experts believed that it would take rescue parties three days to reach the crashed 'plane and the survivors, and might take five; Grayson knew his job.

The village post was collected at six o'clock; at half-past five, after a rush to read the article through and make ink corrections, Canning hurried downstairs. Belle was in the kitchen.

"Coming!" she called.

Canning waited while she took off an apron. She had just finished making pastry; a pie and a dozen small tarts stood ready for the oven.

"We might meet Celia on the way," Belle said.

They went out of the front door, their eyes narrowed against the slanting sun. She looked back once and waved, so Bob was at a window.

"How is he?" Canning asked.

"His shoulder seems easier. Otherwise, he's—just terrified."

"I suppose he is," Canning said wearily. "I think I'm probably crazy, but I'll do it, Belle. We'll give him until to-day week."

When he glanced at her, he saw tears streaming down her face. This *wasn't* Belle; she would no more cry in the road, where neighbours might see her, than she would throw her arms round him and kiss him in Minchester High Street. She fumbled at his pocket, and he knew that she wanted a handkerchief. He gave it to her. She dried her eyes and blew her nose, but didn't speak until they had posted the article and were half-way back. Then:

"I can't say anything, George. I'll make up for it."

Canning muttered: "Forget it," gruffly, and they walked on.

Bob was in the hall when they went in, near the telephone. It was the first time Canning had seen him since the birth of terror in the kitchen. The boy's pallor was alarming, his huge eyes bright with fear, but he had himself under control.

"Celia just 'phoned," he said.

"Is she going to be home late?"

"She might not come home," Bob said. "Matthew—Matthew's staying with the—you know who, to-night. He's awfully cut up. She thinks she'll stay with Peggy, that's near—" he gulped. "That's near Marlborough Road. She said don't worry. I said it would be all right."

"I suppose it's a good thing," Belle said. "She'll be comfortable enough at Peggy's, and it will give you a chance to get over the shock before you see them, Bob." She paused. "Your father is going to wait for a few days, and see what happens."

Bob's eyes lit up with a light which drove fear away.

"Oh, *thanks*."

"How's your shoulder?" asked Belle brusquely. "Is it well enough for you to help me lay the table?"

Canning didn't go into the kitchen, but went up to the study. He hadn't heard Belle so brusque with Bob before. It was her 'no nonsense' voice, often used with Celia; she had been strict but fair with Celia.

Canning felt that he could relax. He was mentally and physically worn out. It might be the wrong decision, but at least he had made it, and could put the problem aside. He was even beginning to think that Belle might be right. Thank God Celia and Matthew weren't coming home. They could all get a grip on themselves, and by to-morrow evening should be able to behave normally. No one would be surprised if Bob were shamefaced and quiet. If Celia hadn't put two and two together by now, there was no reason why she ever should.

There was plenty of work he could do. He started on it, became absorbed, and worked until dinner time. Bob hardly said a word. He seemed more puzzled by his mother than by

Canning. Belle was very matter-of-fact with him. In the past, a bruised finger would have won him freedom from any kitchen chore; now she made him understand that she expected his help. Canning saw the way the boy watched her, as if he too saw a stranger.

Quite suddenly, Canning realized that he felt no sense of burden, no heaviness of spirit. In its place was a sense of exhilaration. He saw it simply as the rebirth of hope that there might be a reconciliation between him and Belle.

All three went into the drawing-room after dinner. It was a long, narrow room of blues and gold, the show-piece of the house. It had comfort as well as charm, and Canning liked the room which was Belle's greatest pride. He read the paper and some weekly reviews. Belle was sewing, Bob sat near the radio, tuned in to light music. The peace upon Canning seemed to touch them all; even Bob had relaxed.

At half-past nine, the telephone bell rang.

"Go and see who that is, Bob," Belle said promptly.

"Yes, mum." Bob got up at once and hurried across the room. Belle watched him, smiling faintly. Canning felt edginess return. He heard Bob speak; there was a pause, then a shrill gasp and stifled scream of:

"*Who?*"

"Oh, dear God!" cried Belle. "What's happened?"

9

REQUEST

BELLE jumped up and flew across the room, with Canning on her heels. With the hall light shining straight on to his face, Bob stood with his mouth open, all the terror back. He couldn't speak. The telephone was in his hand, quivering; his whole body shook.

"*See who it is,*" hissed Belle.

Canning took the receiver. Belle put her arm round Bob's

shoulders, and hustled him back into the drawing-room. A man spoke before Canning got the receiver to his ear.

"What's that?" Canning made himself ask.

"Oh, it's you, George," the man said. "Who on earth answered me just now?"

"My son. I don't know what happened—" Canning was faced with the desperate need to explain away that gasping: "*who?*" He almost choked, but managed to say, "He hurt himself, I think. Who's that?"

"Ted Banfield," the other said.

Canning felt something of the shock which had broken Bob's self-control. His teeth seemed clamped together, but he had to be normal, if he behaved oddly too it might make Banfield wonder. God! Why couldn't he get a grip on himself?

"Sorry—sorry, Ted, I didn't recognize you." Would Banfield have spoken so calmly if this were a part of the inquiry? "What's worrying you?"

"One murder," Banfield said dryly. "Are you busy this evening, George?"

"Well—"

"Because I think you could help. You speak German fluently, don't you?"

"Well—"

Banfield chuckled. "There's no need to be modest, I've just been talking to Randall. He says that you took him and his son on a tour of Germany last year and spoke like a native. You can't speak Polish, by any chance, can you?"

Canning almost shouted. "No!"

"Outlandish language, I'm told." Banfield was in high good humour. "I think German would do. We're holding a chap for questioning. The Dales' gardener. He's a Pole who's only been over here for a few months, and his English isn't so hot. I don't want to make a mistake with his answers. He says he speaks German good! Would you mind coming and acting as interpreter? It's only for the evening, we'll have an official interpreter here to-morrow. I could ask one or two people in town, but it had to be done by someone I can rely on." Banfield obviously took it for granted that the answer would be yes.

"What do you want to question him about?" Canning asked. That was only to gain time, to think. He need not accept. Banfield might be annoyed if he refused, but there could be no compulsion. Trying to decide what to say was torment.

"Why, the murder, obviously," Banfield said. "Of course if you don't feel like playing policeman it doesn't matter, but I can't think of anyone else who'd do half as well."

"I see." Canning knew he would have to go; it was as if fate demanded it; give him a chance to see this Waclow. "Oh, all right, I'll do what I can."

"Good man!" Banfield was pleased. "Come straight to the police station, will you, and just give the sergeant your name. He'll show you straight up to me."

"Right-ho," Canning said. "Good-bye."

He rang off, and stood without moving. There was no sound from the drawing-room; the radio was no longer on. He closed his eyes for a moment, then heard movement. When he opened his eyes, Belle was at the doorway.

"What did he want?" She was sharp again; fearful.

"He needs—" Canning hesitated. "He needs an interpreter, and wants me to go in and see him. I said I'd go." He half expected Belle to shout that he was a fool, he should have refused, but she didn't, just looked at him with her strange, new calm. "I think it would look odd if I didn't. He'd wonder why."

"Perhaps you're right," Belle said. "Go and tell Bob, will you?" She passed him and went into the dining-room.

Canning went in to Bob, who stood by the silent radio, his right hand stiff by his side, his eyes dark and glittering still and enormous. "It was nothing to do with you, Bob."

Bob didn't move.

"They want to question a man in German, and I'm to be the interpreter." Bob still didn't move. "Bob, I promised you that I would wait a few days. Have you ever known me break a promise?"

His son formed the word 'no' but couldn't utter it, moved wildly and flung himself face forward into a chair. He began to sob. Canning felt as if he were imprisoned; there was nothing he could say, nothing he could do. It was a relief when Belle came in, carrying a glass. She glanced at Bob as she thrust the glass into his hand; a little of the contents spilled on to his fingers.

"I thought you'd need a whisky and soda," she said. "Don't worry about him." There was compassion in her gaze as she looked at Bob, but she didn't go towards him. "It will do him good, he's been bottling it up all day. Believe me, he'll be different after this." She spoke as if she meant to make sure.

"Yes," Canning said. "Yes, probably." He sipped. "You didn't waste the soda!" He was glad of the whisky, although it meant that he would break one of his self-imposed rules: never have a drink just before driving. That was part of his continual striving—to live as he believed a man should live. "I don't suppose I'll be late."

"Is it about—the case?"

"Yes."

"No one has any mercy on you, do they?" Belle said with a twisted smile. "Of all the people he could have asked!" She went to a small table and took a cigarette from a box. "Give me a light, George, will you? Have you plenty of cigarettes upstairs?"

"Yes."

"Bob's smoking rather heavily. I suppose we can't blame him, and it helps. Thank God he's never got a taste for whisky like his father!" She was almost gay, but it was a brittle gaiety. Yet something of the old Belle showed, the quality she had passed on to Celia. "If you're not too late, you might find out if Celia's all right."

"I will." Canning sipped again. "The cigarettes are in the bottom left-hand drawer of my desk. Help yourself."

"I'll go and get the car out first," Belle said. "I didn't think we'd need it again to-night, so I put it away."

He watched her go out, moving with that easy grace which

had often hurt because it had reminded him of things as they had been. The front door opened and a breeze swung this door to and fro. Bob's racking sobs had quietened a little, but his shoulders still moved. Canning drank again, slowly, wondering if the boy would turn round before he left. He ought to say something.

"Try not to let it get you down, Bob."

There was no answer.

He couldn't infuse any warmth into his voice, and Bob probably realized that, knew that his father was acting against his better judgment, that he had already condemned. It was better to leave the boy to Belle.

She came back, flushed, her eyes sparkling.

"It's cold out, take your thick coat."

"I will."

"You'd better not keep them waiting too long," Belle said.

Five minutes later Canning was driving towards the gates, which showed up white in the headlights. Belle had opened them. She had been gone longer than he realized; time had lost its meaning. In spite of the thick coat, he was chilled through when he reached the main road. He drove slowly, because of the whisky; that had been a stiff one. The headlights shone on the shimmering telephone wires, on the close hedges and turned them to a silvery green. There was little traffic on the road, but just outside Minchester a fool came round a corner on the wrong side, then wrenched his wheel; there couldn't have been more than an inch or two between the two cars.

It was nearly ten by the Town Hall clock when he turned off the High Street into the narrow road where Police Headquarters were. Two cars stood outside. He left his behind the nearer one, and walked briskly to the steps. A constable there saluted but didn't question him.

A sergeant came from a room on the right of the bleak hall with its stone floor.

"Good evening, sir."

"My name is Canning, and Superintendent—"

"Oh, that's right, sir." The sergeant was elderly, fatherly, amiable. "It's the second door on the right upstairs, think you can find your way up, sir?"

"I think so," Canning said dryly.

Randall had told him about the Pole; once he had recovered from the revulsion against Banfield's request, he had recalled that. He wondered if the suspect would be in Banfield's office, as he tapped at the door.

Banfield was alone in a room which Canning had never entered before. He was surprised to find it so small, although it was bright with fluorescent lighting, and spick and span. A desk which filled half the room was in one corner, and Banfield was getting up from a large padded chair, behind it. Banfield was a hand-shaker, with a big hand and a powerful grip.

"It's very good of you to turn out, George. I can understand you being reluctant. Nothing much the matter with your son, I hope?"

"Eh?"

"Didn't he hurt himself at the telephone?"

"Oh, that, yes! Silly young ass had a knife in his hand," Canning said. The lie was prompted by Banfield's first question, and was smooth and convincing by the time it was uttered. "I can't say that I like the idea of helping to question suspects. I only have to translate, I hope."

"Word for word, if possible," Banfield said. "The fellow's scared stiff, and I mean to have a go at him before he has a night's sleep and feels better! Getting them at the right time is a big factor, you know." He was very self-satisfied, almost smug. "Mind you, it might be fright because he's at the police station, you can never tell with these Europeans, can you?" That marked Banfield as an insular type, which wasn't surprising. His big, long face was shiny, and he blew his nose. "Bit of a cold. I'm not going to say anything more to you at this stage, if you don't mind. All I need—but we've gone into that! Let's go down and see the chap." He rounded the desk. "I'll ask you the questions in English, you just translate and pass them on, then pass his answers back to me. A.B.C., really."

"If my German and his can stand it."

"His wife says that he lived in Germany for years. I feel sorry for her. Little Scots lass." Banfield would always say 'lass' for a Scots girl. His manner could not have said more clearly that he thought he had the killer. "They met in Germany, she was in some billet over there. She knows German well, so does old Dale, who gave them this job. The Pole's proving slow at picking up English," Banfield added.

He led the way along a wide, dimly lit passage to a room at the end, and went in without knocking. It was a barn of a room furnished with several wooden chairs and a table. Three people were there. One was a constable in uniform, another a big man in a navy blue suit, the other, obviously, the Pole.

He sat on an upright chair in a corner of the room. He was quite small; not much bigger than Bob. The thing that struck Canning first was the similarity between his manner and Bob's; the man was terrified. He held himself tautly, watched the newcomers with nervous tension, his eyes darting from one to the other. In a very different way from Bob, he was good-looking; so blond that his hair looked grey, with pale blue eyes, a short nose and sensitive lips. There was a touch of quality about him.

"He hasn't said a word, sir," said the man in plain clothes.

"No change, eh? Well, perhaps he'll get along better now that we've someone who can speak a language he understands properly. By the way, George, his name's Waclow, Stanislaus Waclow. Supposing you try out his German."

Canning said: "All right," and smiled at the Pole. He knew that if there were nothing else on his mind, if the business about Bob were just a bad dream, he would still feel considerable sympathy for this man. He spoke quietly, slowly; there was change in Waclow's manner almost from the first.

"I think you can speak German well, Mr. Waclow."

"German, yes!" The Pole straightened up. "It is my second language." His words poured out. "Will you please tell the policeman it is a great mistake. I was not at the house, I was away from it."

"I'll tell him." Canning translated, briskly.

"So we've overcome the language difficulty," Banfield said with relief. "That's fine. Ask him where he was between half-past eleven and half-past one last night, will you?"

Canning passed the question on.

"I was with friends."

"Ask him to give the names of the friends, and addresses where we can find them," Banfield said.

Canning did so.

"I cannot name them," Waclow said. "I do not know their names." He went on swiftly, before Canning could translate. "They were also Polish, they had worked on a farm and were going to another place, I do not know the name of the place. We were very happy together. Earlier I had talked to them in a public house, where I had a drink with my wife. They came home with me, we drank some more." Canning tried to stop him, but he would not stop, was desperately anxious to tell his story. It came in a torrent. Canning had no experience of distinguishing truth from falsehood, and did not find it hard to believe. Three exiles had met in a pub, and been delighted to talk in their native language. Waclow and his wife were staying with the wife's parents for the 'holiday', and the men had left at eleven o'clock. Waclow had arrived back a little after two. Obviously Banfield had allowed the half-hour to travel from the wife's home, on the outskirts of the town, to Marlborough Road.

When Waclow stopped, his eyes burned with eagerness to be believed.

Canning translated.

"All right," Banfield said. "That's pretty well what we understood before. I want to know exactly where he was."

Waclow couldn't say. He did not know Minchester well. He had walked for some distance. His 'friends' were going to sleep under a hedge. It had been somewhere out of the town, but not far away. They had just talked and gone on talking. He had seen no one on his way back to his wife's home.

"Ah," breathed Banfield. Canning felt that he could actively dislike this man, whom he had respected for years. "If he didn't know where he was, how did he get home so easily?"

Waclow couldn't answer that.

"He says he followed his nose," Canning said. "He knew the middle of the town was in a certain direction and walked for half an hour before he recognized the streets."

Banfield flung question after question, some cunningly framed. Waclow sensed that his answers weren't satisfactory. He seemed to draw into himself. The hope that Canning's arrival had brought vanished completely. The pale, sensitive face and the haunted eyes were pathetic. Canning found himself thinking wildly; he could stop this torture, need only say a dozen words to Banfield, and the Pole would suffer nothing more.

Bob and Belle had been promised—

"All right," Banfield said. "Ask him if he's seen this before, will you?"

He took a knife out of his pocket. It was large, with several blades; an elaborate Boy Scout's knife. Canning sensed that this was something new, to trap the Pole; but that was less important than the probability that this was *the* knife. He stared at it as it was held out towards Waclow, who sat back, hands raised over it.

"Have you seen that before?"

The Pole made no attempt to deny that the knife was his, but sight of it obviously shocked him. Dully, he said he had lost it a week ago. Canning thought that, from this moment, Waclow sensed that he was trapped.

Canning felt that he could not go on any longer.

"Ask him how much money was in his room—the one in his in-laws' home," Banfield said.

Canning put the question.

"There is no money," Waclow said.

Canning began: "Ted, I'm sorry, but—"

"That'll do for now, I think. Tell him we shall hold him for the night, will you? If he isn't willing to stay, I'll charge him."

Canning said: "All right." He told Waclow rather more; that he was being held for further questioning and that there was no charge against him yet. The man took the blow with a fatalism that was hurtful. He watched Banfield, not Canning, as they went out.

10

CELIA

THE passage struck bleak and cold. Canning shivered. Banfield stode towards his own office, and thrust open the door. The light was on, much brighter than that in the passage or the room where they had questioned the prisoner.

"You've earned a drink," Banfield said heartily, and closed the door before going over to his big desk. He seemed on top of the world. "What did you make of that chap, George?"

"I felt sorry for him."

Banfield grinned.

"I'll bet he feels sorry for himself, but not so sorry as he will later! Just between you and me, I think it's open and shut, now. Lost the knife, did he? Never was much doubt." Banfield bent down to a cupboard in the corner behind his desk and took out a bottle of whisky, a syphon and two glasses. "Anything I say is in confidence, of course. That's why I wanted you to come, no certainty that some people won't go and blurt what they've heard all over the place, and there are several London newspapermen in town. I don't want to blot my copy book." Whisky gurgled into the glasses. "As soon as I've had a word with the Chief Constable, I'll charge Waclow. Say when." He squirted soda from a syphon.

"When, thanks. So you're sure he did it."

"I'd be surprised if there's any doubt," Banfield said.

"Cheers!" As he drank, he looked like a big cart-horse. "No need to call in Scotland Yard, and a pat on the back for yours truly! Mind you, I'll try to find these 'friends' he talked about, but even if they exist, they were probably in the job with him. And if they weren't, they'd lie."

"Aren't you rather assuming guilt?" Canning forced the question.

"Simply making deductions from the evidence," Banfield said, he beamed. "He can't really account for his movements, he and his wife knew that the Dales kept money at the house, and that Dale had won a lot at the races on Saturday. Waclow probably saw him put it away—they left for this holiday on Sunday morning. Anyhow, you don't know everything, George. There's more than that, and more than proof that the knife used was Waclow's."

Canning was glad to sit down.

"Shouldn't really tell you," Banfield went on, leaning against the desk. "We found fifty pounds in one-pound notes at Waclow's house—that is, the house where he's staying. His wife can't account for it, she says she didn't know he had any money. And Jerry Dale's fingerprints are on some of the notes! No wonder Waclow denied knowing about it." Banfield finished his drink. "If the Public Prosecutor can't get a conviction on that, he's falling down on his job. Like another?"

"No, thanks. I ought to be going. I promised my wife I'd have a word with Celia before going back, and make sure she's all right. She's staying with—"

"She's at the Dales' house, or I miss my guess," Banfield told him. "I'd just come from there—and she was with Matthew Grant, Jerry and old Dale. Mrs. Dale's prostrate. Dreadful shock. You might think of them when you feel sorry for Waclow, George! It's too easy to forget the victims and the sufferers, you know."

Canning didn't speak.

"Like me to telephone and find out if she's still there?" asked Banfield.

"Thanks. I'd like a word with her." Canning would have

gone to her friend's house, but would not go to the Dales'. A meeting with old Dale, whom he knew slightly, and Jerry and Matthew, was the last thing he wanted. He wouldn't be able to face them.

As Banfield put in the call, Canning was picturing Waclow's face, and thinking of the fifty pounds. That was the first thing that had really given him hope. If the Pole had stolen that money, there was surely a chance that he had actually committed the murder. Here was an indication, if nothing stronger, that he had also broken into the house. Anything which could throw doubt on Bob's guilt could be vital. Banfield seemed so sure that he had the right man, and undoubtedly the knife was Waclow's. According to Bob, Peter Dale—well, the man he had knocked out, obviously Peter Dale—had produced the knife. What would Peter have been doing with a knife owned by the gardener and odd-job man? Was there another knife?

Canning hadn't the courage to ask.

"Is Miss Canning there?" Banfield was asking. "Ask her to speak to her father, will you? Here you are, George." He held out the receiver.

"Thanks." Canning took it, and a moment later Celia came on the line.

"Hallo, Dad, where are you?"

"I'm at the police station."

"Why on earth are you there?"

"The police had a language problem," Canning said, and infused some warmth into his voice. "Your mother was anxious about you, and I promised to make sure you were all right. You won't stay there too long, will you?"

"As a matter of fact I shall probably stay the night," Celia said. "Jerry's mother is dreadfully upset, and I may be able to help. Perhaps you'd better not tell Mother, though!" She almost laughed. "She'll only worry, and I'll be all right. Dad—"

"Yes?"

"I felt beastly about the way I talked to you this morning."

"Forget it," Canning said. "Well, I suppose you're old enough to know what you're doing, and if you can help Mrs. Dale you may as well stay there. How's Matt?"

"He's all right—just a minute, Dad." She went off the line, Canning waited, watching Banfield pour himself out another whisky and soda. Banfield, on the other side of the desk, began to read some notes. There were voices in the background, Celia's and a man's, presumably Matt's. Then: "Dad, Matt says can you spare him five minutes."

Canning didn't answer; dislike of talking to Matt about the murder amounted almost to dread.

"Are you there?" Celia asked urgently.

"Yes, I—"

"Matt wants a word with you, here you are." There was another pause, before Matthew spoke quietly. His voice sounded very deep over the telephone:

"Hallo, Mr. Canning. I know it's late, but as you're in town, I really would like five minutes' chat. Do you mind?"

There was no reason why Canning should mind; no excuse he could think of to refuse. Why did Matthew want to see him, though? Or did he mean a talk over the telephone?

"Won't the 'phone do, Matthew?"

"Well, no," Matthew said apologetically, "Could you look in here? It's on the way home, only a few yards out of your way. Of course, if you're dead beat—" Matthew broke off.

If he refused, Matthew would wonder why and Celia might also start wondering, and Canning did not want them to probe deeply. The possibility that they would connect Bob's late homecoming with the murder was all too real, and he couldn't convince himself that it was because of what he knew. He wanted to find out what Matthew wanted, too.

"All right," he said. "I'm leaving at once."

"Thanks very much," Matthew said. "Good-bye."

Canning rang off, and Banfield looked up from his notes; he was no longer smiling, and seemed preoccupied.

"Everything all right?"

"Yes, thanks. I'll be going."

"Very helpful of you to come," Banfield said, and stood up. "Mum's the word, of course. I'm just wondering whether I should go and see the Chief Constable now, or wait until the morning." He shook hands. "If we should need you again, you'll come, won't you?"

Canning said sharply: "I thought you would have an official interpreter by the morning."

"Well, I hope to, old chap, but in a case like this you never know what might crop up. I won't worry you any more than I have to, believe me." Banfield still wasn't really with him, and opened the door. "Good night, and warmest thanks. I really mean that."

Canning went out, and shivered as wind swept up the stairs from the open door. The sergeant was still at his desk, just inside the room, and made to get up.

"Good night, sir."

"Good night."

It was much colder outside, and since Canning had arrived a wind had sprung up; either that, or he hadn't noticed it before. He went to the car. It was ten minutes' drive to Marlborough Street; he knew it well, because in a house near the Dales' was a private museum and a library, maintained by a trust for the interest of Minchester townsfolk; he often used the library. The side streets were deserted, and the lighting was poor. As he drove, very cautiously, figures loomed up out of the darkness on either side. A cyclist without lights cut round a corner, and made him jam on his brakes suddenly. Soon he was in the wide streets, with houses standing in their own extensive grounds on either side. Most of the houses here were Victorian, with a few late Georgian beauties; the Dales' was one of these. Canning wasn't quite sure which one it was, hadn't thought to check the name or the number; that exasperated him. He drove slowly, and stopped at the gates of a house where there were lights upstairs and down. He still wasn't sure that this was the right one, but got out and approached it. A car showed up against the front room light, and a moment later he saw that it was Matthew's green sports car, an M.G. Canning went back for his own car.

The front garden was large, with a shrubbery on one side, thick and dark, a plot of grass in the middle, and a circular drive; Matthew's car was parked on one side of this. There was no sound when Canning switched off his engine. He didn't get out at once, but sat looking at the two round, grey pillars and the wide porch. Which window had Bob used to climb in?

The damned young *fool.*

He opened the door and got out, as the front door of the house opened. Matthew appeared, tall and dark against the bright light, and Celia was just behind him. Matthew came forward hurriedly.

"We thought we heard the car. It *is* good of you to come." He waited at the top of the three steps, and Celia joined him; she linked her arm in his. "I hope you won't want to curse me when you hear what it's all about."

It was impossible to judge anything from his expression, and Celia seemed quite calm. So it couldn't be a question about Bob. As they went into the spacious hall, furnished with antiques which Canning knew to be worth a fortune, he felt like turning and running away. He must keep his nerve. Why should he be so edgy, anyhow? The truth would have to come out; even if Waclow had killed Peter Dale, Bob's part would have to be told. He'd only promised to keep quiet for a week, and Belle and Bob knew that the truth might come out before then.

Matthew closed the door.

Jerry Dale came from a room on the right. The electric light made his face seem even pastier than it had in the street, his eyes were red-rimmed and glassy; he looked like a man who would soon collapse. But for his complexion, he would have been good-looking in a rather flabby way. His thin black hair was plastered down, his small red mouth was set tightly.

"You met Jerry this morning, didn't you?" Matthew said.

"Yes."

" 'Fraid I was a bit preoccupied," Jerry said, and came forward, forcing a smile. That made him look more attractive; almost babyish. Of course, he was very young; all of them were young, little more than children. His voice had a curious tone, too warming, friendly. "Very good of you to come over."

There was no reason to think that they had anything on their minds about Bob. As Canning felt relief, he also felt tired and old. Yet he had to keep alert.

"It's warmer in here," Jerry went on. He ushered Canning into a small room, with a door communicating with the room next door. This room had a fine, high ceiling, a rich red carpet, heavy velvet curtains. Against one wall was an old court cupboard, Jacobean and beautifully carved. It had a dull surface which somehow shone a little; a collector's gem which might have secret compartments. Was this the room in which Bob had found the money? Had the fight with Peter been here? There were no signs of a disturbance, but then there had been time to tidy up. Yet wouldn't the police be in charge of the room where the body was discovered?

"Do let me get you a drink Mr. Canning." Jerry was forcing himself to be amiable; why? He looked a sick man.

"No, thanks," Canning said. "I—"

"Daddy makes a rule of never drinking when he's going to drive," Celia broke in lightly. She looked completely at home here, calmer and more self-possessed than either of the men; more truly, perhaps, she showed no signs of strain. "Sit down, Dad."

There was a large, winged armchair drawn up near the glowing coal fire in the big fireplace, probably an Adam.

"Now what's all this about?" Canning asked.

Matthew stood a few feet away from him, Jerry waited, watching the older man closely, tensely; even Celia looked at him as if a great deal depended on what he said.

"As you can imagine, Jerry's pretty worked up," Matthew said quietly. "The police aren't exactly communicative, and he—well, all of us for that matter—would like to know whether they've arrested the gardener, Waclow. As you were there over a language problem, I assumed it was because of Waclow, whose English isn't very good. Is there anything—"

Jerry moved forward abruptly, raised his clenched hands.

"I can't rest until I know they've caught the swine. Was it Waclow? That's all we want to know."

11

NIGHT

THE answer was vital to them, and none could guess Canning's own mental torment. The viciousness in Jerry Dale's voice was understandable; and it revealed to Canning much more than Jerry's frame of mind. It made him aware of the stricken woman upstairs, and old Dale, the father, who must feel almost as stricken. It brought home the tragedy which had come with stunning suddenness to the whole family. There was more, too; memory of Waclow's tense face, and the way he had turned when he had seen the knife and guessed what it seemed to imply.

"Easy, Jerry," Matthew said. "We know that anything the police told you was in confidence, Mr. Canning, but—"

"I just want to know. I shan't say a word to anyone else." Jerry was less abrupt, almost pleading.

"There isn't much I can tell you," Canning said. "I did interpret for the police, but it didn't amount to much. Just an account of Waclow's movements last night. Obviously I can't tell you what was said, but I can tell you that Waclow's still at the police station."

"So he did it," Jerry breathed.

"It's too early to say that, I think." Canning hardly knew how to satisfy them and also cut short his own ordeal. "I have a feeling that Banfield will probably make up his mind what to do in the morning. If I were you, I'd try to get some sleep, Mr. Dale. I don't think there's any way you can help."

"If I thought the killer was still free I'd work night and day to get him!" The band-leader was almost hysterical. There was little doubt that Matthew had asked Canning to come in the hope of calming him down.

"Of course you would." Canning tried to soothe. "Banfield seems satisfied, I think I can tell you that. You should have the full story in the morning." He stood up. "I must be getting back, my wife will wonder what's become of me." It wouldn't surprise Belle if he were back very late, but he was desperately eager to get away. "Decided what you're going to do, Celia?"

"Stay here," she said promptly. "I'm going to sleep in the room next to Mrs. Dale. I might be able to help her. Will you tell Mother?" She was anxious—as if she knew that Belle would disapprove; Canning hadn't realized before how guarded Celia was about Belle. There had never been anything like a conspiracy between him and his daughter; and this was a mild form.

He forced a smile. "I don't see any need to, but I can't see that it matters much, anyhow. Good night, my dear." She came forward, and he kissed her cheek—and realized that he would miss seeing her in the morning. "Don't come out again, it's cold."

"All right. Good night, Dad."

"Good night, Mr. Canning," Jerry said. "Sorry if I let off steam a bit."

"I can quite understand," Canning said.

Only Matthew saw him to his car, and was silent until they reached it. The wind howled among the trees and through the shrubbery.

"Nasty night," Matthew said at last. "Sorry I brought you out, but I fancied it might help Jerry a little if he thought that the police had really got a move on. He's—well, you can see what it's done to him. What it's done to us all, for that matter. There wasn't a finer chap than Peter. We—that is, Celia and I—know the family well, of course, and Mrs.

Dale just felt that she would like Celia around. Everything will be all right."

"I'm sure it will be."

"How's Bob?" Matthew asked. He had a way of making everything he said seem sincere, no matter how trivial; he sounded now as if he really cared how Bob was, although he did not know him well and could not have formed a good impression.

"Oh, he's all right."

"Peter rather took to him," Matthew said. "He thought that he might make a good trumpeter if he really put his back into it. I thought he was going to, for a while, he was always at rehearsals—Jerry's band, you know. He'll be cut up about Peter."

Canning didn't speak. He should have said that Bob was shocked, upset; he couldn't bring himself to say a word.

Matthew didn't dwell on the subject.

"Good night, sir."

" 'Night, Matthew." Canning switched on the headlights. Matthew stood back. Canning drove out and turned right when he should have turned left. It took him some minutes to get back on the right road, and the headlights carved avenues of light through the dark, wide streets, shining on the tall trees which enshrouded most of the houses. This was a notorious neighbourhood for buglary, for the wealthier people of the town congregated here. He could picture Bob walking along, creeping—no, he had cycled. A cyclist passed on the other side of the road, Where was *he* going? Motorists might have passed Bob like that, and wouldn't have given him a thought. He could imagine Bob hiding the bicycle and getting into the grounds. He had planned it all so carefully, and it was worse because he had known the Dales and they had been friendly, encouraging; the more Canning learned about it, the less sympathy he could find for his son.

But there was the little matter of justice, of getting at the truth. It was still possible that Bob was not a murderer. What was the proper thing to do?

Canning wasn't thinking of telling the police about it yet,

that was all settled. But should he encourage Bob, and that really meant Belle, to think that someone else might actually have done the killing?

If Waclow were arrested the news would soon be out. The belief that he wouldn't be accused of murder after all might persuade Bob to give himself up.

Canning drove very slowly.

He knew at heart that he was deceiving himself—nothing would persuade Bob to go to the police. Belle was fooling herself if she really thought he would. Did she? Was she expecting or at least hoping for a miracle? If her outlook had actually changed, if the disaster had broken through the years of hatred, then she might seriously think that Bob could have changed, too.

Was she seeing things differently?

Or was this a deliberately thought-out plan, to make him hold his hand, Canning wondered. Belle knew him well, knew how desperately he was tormented. And he kept reminding himself that she was no fool.

The twisting road unfurled in front of him. There was practically no traffic about. Soon he came within sight of the lamp at the corner of his road. The garage there was closed. He turned off, and forgot to change gear; the engine nearly stalled. He pulled into the side and stopped, switched the headlights off, and lit a cigarette.

If he were honest with himself, he would admit that he hadn't an iota of faith in his son, was fully prepared to believe the worst about him. Bob was past redemption. Borstal, and the prisons were full of youths who had started as he had, whom nothing had changed. No, his hope lay in Belle.

The true reason why he had not run away was that he was still in love with her. She could stir him deeply. Even to-day, her body, with its slender beauty, could cast a spell. In their worst moments, Belle could fool him, make him believe that there was hope; and there had been times when he had felt as if she had seduced him. Was the truth simply that he couldn't live without her? Had she taken possession of him, warping his mind, corrupting his principles, commanding his body?

Whatever had happened in the past, there *was* hope that she had now realized that she had been wrong; and that in gratitude for the chance he was giving Bob, she would change completely. The very thought of that hurt—like the promise of water to a man dying of thirst, who saw it, stretched out a hand yet knew when his fingers closed about the vessel, it would vanish. But he had to try; out of evil cometh good. Out of Bob's crime might come the mending of broken years.

Canning tossed the cigarette out of the window, started the engine and drove on. There was still a light in the drawing-room, so Belle hadn't gone to bed.

The front door opened as he went up the drive. The garage doors were already open; he waved and drove straight in. When he got to the doors, Belle was already closing one. He shut the other, and turned the key in the padlock. When they turned away, Belle linked her arm in his. She was wearing a black fur coat, which was eight years old. He knew that only too well; she had reminded him about it, spitefully, a few weeks ago—gibing that he couldn't afford even to clothe his wife properly. The fur was snug against his bare hand. The coat suited her, and her fair hair was like a crown.

"You're cold," she said. "I've made a good fire."

"We ought to go to bed."

"You can have a warm through first." They entered the hall, and Canning closed and locked the door. She loosened her coat; beneath it she wore a pale green housecoat which clung to her figure. He helped her off with the fur, and they went into the drawing-room; Bob wasn't there.

"He's gone to bed," Belle said. "I gave him one of my sleeping tablets. He must have plenty of sleep."

"How was he?"

"Terrified," she said frankly. "But he had one consolation, he knew that you wouldn't go back on your word." She took her arm away from Canning's and went to the fireplace. By the side of his chair was the whisky and soda, and a trolley was drawn up with sandwiches, biscuits and tea things; a kettle sung on a hob specially fitted, another of her little economies. The fire drew him, warming him through. "What was it all about, George?"

He needn't tell her, but knew that he would. He was determined that he would not tell her everything, only enough to make her think that he had. Once she thought that, she wouldn't ask many questions.

"They've detained the gardener who worked for the Dales. A Pole—he speaks English badly, but has fluent German."

"Oh," said Belle, very flatly.

"I didn't enjoy it much," Canning said wearily, and dropped into his chair. "I had to interpret all the police questions. The man can't account for his movements last night. Banfield was very cautious, wouldn't let me know too much. I think that he seriously suspects the chap."

"Oh," repeated Belle. She looked at him straightly. "And you still didn't tell Banfield what you know?"

Canning closed his eyes. "No."

"How you must have hated it!" Belle said. She poured him out a whisky. When he looked, her expression was strange—soothing and yet puzzling. She was calm, even serene, and very like Celia. It made her look younger and took his mind back nearly twenty years. Her hair looked pretty, too, fluffier than usual. "Sandwich?" She pulled up a pouf, sat down, and lifted a plate from the trolley. "It's nearly one o'clock, you must be hungry."

"Thanks. Yes, I hated it."

"Bob will confess," she said softly. "I feel sure he will, George; I feel sure it will be too much for him to keep silent." Canning was now quite convinced that she was fooling herself. "All of this will be worth while, before it's finished. Did you—did you manage to find out any more details? Have they any idea that anyone else was there?"

"I don't think so."

"If they think this gardener—" she broke off abruptly. "What's the use of talking about that? Did you see Celia?"

"I telephoned her, she's all right." The fire and the

whisky were warming him, and the torment of his mind eased. He relaxed physically, and calm stole upon him, a contentment which he seldom found except while working, or in the garden or, occasionally, in Minchester with his friends.

There was a lot he could tell Belle; about how well Bob knew the Dales, for instance, and how the victim's family was affected, but what was the use? He realized how tired he was, and the fire made his eyes heavy. Belle didn't harass him. She made tea for herself, and when he had finished his whisky, stretched out for his glass, He stirred.

"No more. You'll soon have me thinking that you approve of the stuff!"

She smiled, and it touched her eyes.

"Looking back, the marvel is that I didn't drive you to being a dipsomaniac, darling. Ready for bed?" Her eyes were an invitation, and she covered his hand with hers. "There's no need to get up early in the morning, no one to get breakfast for."

"That's something," he said. The new mood was still upon him, and she stood very near, as if inviting him to take her in his arms. He held her arms, tightly, and looked into her eyes, and there was no coldness in them; nor was there the fire of passion, of need, which he knew well. "Belle," he said hoarsely, "don't go back, stay like you are. For God's sake, don't go back!"

"I won't," she said, and her body yielded against him, promising complete surrender. Or demanding it?

Later, he was physically tired and his mind was dulled. Belle lay beside him, breathing evenly, although he could not be sure that she was asleep. He lay on his back with her head on his arm; he would have to move, soon. He didn't sink into sleep. Pins and needles began to steal along his arm, and he moved it as gently as he could. Belle stirred but didn't speak. He turned on his side, and slid his arm round her, his hand upon her breast. Sleep was suddenly a long way off. After a while, he turned round. He needed sleep, but it wasn't surprising that he couldn't get off. He didn't want to wake Belle, but he would have to read a book. He sat up slowly, and pushed his pillow behind him, then stretched out his hand for the bedside lamp. As he touched it, he saw a light come on, showing beneath the door.

It came from the landing.

He stared, listening intently, and thought that he heard stealthy sounds. Bob, of course; weren't the sleeping tablets working?

A suspicion sprang into his mind, and he had to act on it, couldn't keep still any longer. He put on the light and got out of bed; Belle stirred again. He rounded the bed, without troubling to get his dressing-gown, and opened the door cautiously. The light was still on, and Bob's door was wide open. He went towards the head of the stairs, and saw Bob nearly at the bottom, fully dressed, hat and coat on. So the suspicion was justified, and he was right; Bob meant to run away.

He waited tensely, for the boy to glance round.

12

THE STRUGGLE

CANNING felt sure that his son would turn round, so he did not move, just waited as if willing the boy to realize that he was there.

Bob reached the hall. He paused for a moment with a hand on the newel post, then turned to look upstairs. He was moving slowly; when he saw his father, he became absolutely still. The light shone obliquely on to him. It gave his narrow features a shifty, cunning look; it would be easy to call him ugly. *His* son? They seemed a world apart. The silence which fell about them seemed filled with the thunder of an approaching storm.

Canning moved first, and spoke very quietly.

"Keep quiet, your mother's asleep." He started downstairs. Bob turned swiftly and made for the front door; Canning heard the catch in his breath. Canning began to hurry, trying to move silently, tiptoe on his bare feet. Bob pulled at the chain, freed it, and snatched at the bolt; but it was stiff, and jammed. Canning reached the hall. Bob turned round, suddenly; he looked like a cornered rat, crouching with his right shoulder thrust forward.

"Keep away from me!"

"It's no use, Bob." Canning felt no anger. "If you run away, you'll have the police after you."

"I'm leaving, *keep away from me*."

Anger flared.

"Keep your voice down!" Canning went nearer. The boy's lips were parted, and stretched tightly; his white teeth just showed. Had he looked like this when he had fought Peter Dale? "Now come here and be—"

"*Keep away!*"

Canning went on, but more slowly, warily.

"Bob, if you run away—"

His son flew at him.

Canning should have expected it, but the rush was swifter than he thought possible. Bob hurtled against him, right hand raised. Canning felt the hard, tight first on his chin, and staggered back. Bob struck at him again, ferociously, battered his face and sent him reeling against the banisters. The rain of blows stopped. Tears of pain filled Canning's eyes and blurred his vision, and he was gasping; but he heard the sharp sound as the bolt was suddenly released. Pain seemed to fall away. He gathered himself up and went forward. He could just see the boy, half in, half out of the door. He clutched desperately and caught a sleeve. Bob swore, and tore himself free, but in doing so he slipped and fell back against the porch wall.

Canning thrust the door back. It banged. Light fell fully on his son's face and body. Bob tried to dodge away, but was too late. Canning caught him by the arm and pulled him forward savagely, yanked him over the threshold, then flung him away. Bob went down; the hall seemed to shake. Canning pushed the door to, and the wind caught and slammed it A picture rattled on the wall.

Bob crouched on the floor, looking up, fear taking away some of the viciousness. He cringed back as Canning moved.

"Get up."

The boy stayed where he was.

"Get up, you little beast. I ought to thrash you until—" Canning bit on the words, he mustn't let his rage take complete control over him. As they glared, and before either spoke, a sound came from the stairs. Belle, of course; the noise had woken her. Canning didn't look round, but heard her movements. She came into sight, on his left.

Bob began to get up.

"He—" he began shrilly.

"I don't want to hear anything from you," Belle said. "Go up to your room and get into bed." She might have been talking to a schoolboy. There was no edge to her voice, just the flatness of authority.

"Mum, I must get away, I—" Bob's words were strangled.

"You heard what I said, Robert."

He was on his feet now, and moved sideways towards the foot of the stairs. Canning expected him to rush towards the kitchen, and moved to block his path. Perhaps Bob realized there was no escape that way. He backed up the stairs, looking at his mother beseechingly; it seemed to Canning that the boy could not believe that she had turned against him.

Bob reached the landing before he turned round; his door closed, quietly. Belle took Canning's arm.

"You must bathe your face, George."

"I'm all right. And what's the use of sending him up there? He'll climb out of the window, and be away before we know what's happened. We ought to lock him up in the cupboard under the stairs." Canning hardly knew what he was saying, rage tore at him so.

"He won't climb out of the window." Belle was quietly confident. "Come up to the bathroom." She took Canning's arm and went a step ahead of him, up the stairs. At the landing she went straight to Bob's door.

"Robert?"

The boy didn't answer.

She turned the handle and pushed, but the door didn't open. That didn't surprise Canning, but it seemed to nonplus Belle; that was his mistake, for she drew back and said very clearly:

"Robert, if you run away, I shall telephone the police, tell them what happened, and make sure that they start looking for you immediately. I mean that." She turned away quickly. "Come on, George."

When he looked into the bathroom mirror, still marvelling at the way Belle had spoken and at the shrewdness of the threat, Canning was unpleasantly surprised. There were scratches on his cheek and his lips and nose were bleeding; blood spattered his pyjama jacket. He turned the cold tap on. Belle took the sponge before he could reach it, and made him sit down on the bathroom stool. Five minutes later, he looked more presentable. The scratch wasn't much. His nose felt puffy and his lip sore, but he didn't think there would be much to show for it next day. He dabbed his face gingerly with a towel, and the bleeding started again at his lip.

"I'll cauterize that," Belle said, in the practical voice which meant business. The wound stung, but that soon eased. "I think it will be all right, soon. I think we ought to go back to bed. He won't run away now."

She was probably right.

They went into the bedroom, Canning first, Belle switching off the lights; a light shone under Bob's door. It was nearly three o'clock, and Canning felt physically exhausted but his mind was clear. Now that he had come to blows with the boy, it told him just how remote they were from each other; strangers, enemies.

They had always been enemies.

"You'd better have one of my tablets," Belle said.

"They didn't work with him."

"He probably didn't swallow it," Belle said resignedly. "I thought he had." She shook a pink tablet out of a small bottle. "One, or two?"

"I don't know that I want—"

"One or two, that's your only choice."

"Oh, all right, one. What about you?"

"I'll be all right," Belle said. "It won't do me any harm to be awake, for a change." Her smile was wry, taut. She gave him the tablet and fetched him a glass of water. "And no tricks from you, swallow it! You look as if you haven't slept for weeks. Thank goodness the others won't be here in the morning." She waited until he was in bed, and tucked in the bedclothes. "It isn't any use saying I'm sorry, George. I'm beginning to wonder whether I'm right."

It would have been easy to burst out: "No, you're not, he'll never give himself up!" But that wouldn't help. If he did what she considered the right thing by Bob, then the miracle with her might come about. Canning was sliding into full belief in her sincerity.

He said: "He's so frightened, he doesn't know what to do with himself. Would you—would you go to the police if he ran away?"

"Of course I should. He knows it. And if he doesn't, he soon will."

"He might put it to the test, thinking you'd never do it."

She looked down, smiling at him; only the bedside light was on, and it softened her features.

"I don't think he will," she said. "If he has gone in the morning, you can tell your friend Banfield and I won't say a word of complaint. Try to relax, George. You must get some sleep. You may not realize it, but you're not so young as you were!"

He turned on his side, and would have his back to her when she got into bed. Soon, she slid in beside him. He knew that she was lying on her back. He heard her even breathing but was sure that she had not been drowsy when she had laid down. Would the sleeping tablet send him off? He doubted it, he had never felt more wakeful.

He began to doze.

Yes, it was working, he would sleep. He was already relaxed. It was a bewildering situation; when he ought to feel at his worst, tormented because of his own failure, he felt this strange, almost sensuous contentment. He was floating out of the world. He realized now that nothing mattered provided he could win Belle back; why hadn't he realized that before? Perhaps he had, subconsciously. He was going off, beautifully, perfectly.

Then he had a swift, stabbing thought which drove sleep away. He stiffened. Belle did not show that she noticed it, but she must have. He could feel her side against his back, warm, snug; but all contentment had gone. It was a horrible thought, he had no right to let it linger, must get it out of his mind. But how easy it would be for her to drug him. If she were staging a great deception so as to put his mind at rest, and make him think that she was on his side, how easy it would be!

"What's the matter, George?"

"Er—nothing."

"You ought to have had two tablets," Belle said. "I can't get off, I think I'll have one. I'll put the light on for a moment." She sat up. Canning didn't turn round, but heard her fumbling for the bottle, and taking the screw-cap off; then he felt her body move, as it would if she tossed her head back to swallow the tablet. Next moment she did exactly the same; she was drinking, she always kept a glass of water by the side of the bed.

So she had taken a tablet, too.

What put spiteful thoughts like that into a man's head? Why shouldn't he accept the miracle? Why fight against it, as he had fought almost from the beginning?

He felt drowsiness creeping over him again.

When he woke, it was broad daylight; and after the first few seconds, he realized that the sun was high and very bright. It was warm, too. He found that he had only one blanket and the sheet on him. Belle had taken off the other blanket and the eiderdown. Without glancing round he knew she wasn't there but he did glance at her table. The small bottle of sleeping tablets was there but not the glass of water. He was quickly back on the same line of thought; why couldn't be believe that the thing he wanted desperately was coming about? Why fight?

Then he wondered if Bob had stayed; and had his answer when the telephone bell rang, and Bob answered it. He recognized the boy's voice but could not catch the words. Soon, he heard Belle speak, and she apparently had to repeat what she said; he heard:

"Who is it? Answer me!"

There was no answer audible to Canning; the telephone bell gave a faint ting! as the receiver was replaced. Belle spoke again and her voice sounded sharp. Soon afterwards her footsteps sounded on the stairs.

Canning was heavy-headed and still tired; this beginning to the morning did little to cheer him up, but he felt his heart beating faster as Belle drew near. He watched the door. Her footsteps stopped, but the door opened slowly and without a sound. Her bright head appeared round the door.

"Oh, you're awake." She came in briskly, looking at him searchingly. "You don't look *too* bad. Good morning." She came round to his side but didn't kiss him, bent down to put the bedroom kettle on, and then began to tidy the room. "Did you hear the telephone?'

"I heard it ring. '

"Bob had a call from someone, and it scared him," Belle said. She was folding up her flimsy night-dress, and didn't look at Canning. He felt that she was almost frightened by what had happened on the telephone. "He wouldn't tell me who it was. If it had been the police, he would have. I – listen!"

She raised her head. There was a faint ring again, at the telephone. She stepped swiftly to the door, speaking very softly. "He's making a call." Canning thrust the bedclothes back and got out of bed, but before he reached her, she was on the landing. When he got to the door, she had gone into the study, where there was an extension. Canning followed. Belle sat at his desk, quite calmly, with the receiver at her ear. He could hear muttering downstairs; Bob was keeping his voice low, hoping not to be heard. Canning itched to listen-in, but there was nothing he could do.

The call didn't last long.

Belle put down the receiver, looked into Canning's eyes, and then out of the window. This had upset her. Her lips set tightly, and her hand clenched and unclenched on his desk. She might not tell him exactly what she had heard, and he desperately wanted to know. He wouldn't ask—she must volunteer the story. Then she turned her gaze on him again, and her eyes were feverishly bright.

"Someone else knows he was at the Dales' house," she said in a thin voice. "Robert promised to get the money somehow and take it to him." She raised both hands, clenched, in front of her breast; this was the first set-back to her new serenity. "That means he's being blackmailed. Why don't the devils let him alone?"

Canning said hoarsely: "Did you find out who it was?"

"No." She stood up. "No, but I'm going to, I'm going to talk to Robert and if he doesn't tell me the truth I'll shake it out of him." She made for the door.

Canning grabbed her arm.

"Steady, Belle!"

She swung round on him, her eyes blazing; he felt the sickness of disappointment because the other, hysterical Belle was so close again. But he didn't let her go. He didn't try to assess the significance of this, only felt the urgent need to calm her down.

"I'm going to make him tell me the truth, and if he doesn't—"

"Belle, we have to think twice about everything we do," Canning said. His grip was very tight on her arm. "Don't talk to Bob yet. If we're going to have any success, he'll have to confide in us." Belle didn't slacken, was still furiously angry. The irony of what he said didn't occur to him until much later. "It's no use raving at him. If he doesn't get any sympathy from either of us, it will only make him hostile and drive him away."

After a long pause, Belle's tension slackened. She freed herself and went out of the study but into the bedroom. The kettle was boiling. She made tea, while Canning put on his dressing-gown. She brought the tray across to him when he sat down in the armchair which had his clothes draped over the back.

"So you can say that," she said, in an unsteady voice. "Things *have* altered, haven't they?" She sat on the dressing-table stool, her hands folded in her lap. She wore an old, dark red dress, high at the neck and with long sleeves. Her hands, long, smooth and very white in spite of so much housework, seemed relaxed. "After what happened last night." She smiled, slowly, hurtfully. "Look at yourself in the mirror, George."

He bent sideways to do that. His lip was swollen and there was a scratch at one side; other scratches on his cheek were dark with dried blood.

"He's beside himself," Canning muttered. "If we're going to knock any sense into him, we'll have to calm him down first. I don't think this is the time for raving at him. That might come, but not yet."

She handed him his tea, and sipped her own.

"Perhaps you're right," she said, "I'd better—"

A ring at the front-door bell broke across her words. She became stiff again, then put her cup down slowly, went to the window and glanced out, but obviously saw no one, and moved quickly towards the door.

"I'll see who it is." She went out, all her fears betrayed in her nervousness.

Canning went to the head of the stairs, to try to hear what followed.

13

QUESTIONS

"GOOD morning," a man said. "Is Mr. George Canning in?" It was the voice of a stranger, but Canning didn't know whether that was good or bad. He could just see Belle's shapely legs; nothing else. She replied quickly; nothing in the appearance of the caller made her sound at all nervous.

"He's very busy," she said. "Why do you want to see him?"

"I'm from the *Daily Clarion*. You might call me a fellow journalist." The other wasn't ingratiating, just sounded friendly. "I won't keep him long."

"Can I tell him what you want to see him about?" Belle asked. She knew, of course; was just gaining time. The Press had got round to him, probably because he had been to see the Pole last night. What would Belle say? How could she send the man away without causing offence? Her mind must be in turmoil. What of Bob? He was probably at a door downstairs, listening; and the name of the *Daily Clarion* would probably affect him almost as badly as the name of Superintendent Banfield.

"I'd like to see if he can tell me a little more about the Polish gardener who's been charged with murder in the town," the reporter said. "I do assure you that I won't keep him long."

Belle seemed to stand looking at the reporter for a long time. She was probably thinking: "The Pole's been charged with the murder"; and if she stared at the man much longer, he would begin to wonder what worried her.

She spoke at last.

"I'll speak to my husband. Will you come in?"

Canning backed away, but was able to see her as she showed the reporter into the drawing-room. He heard her ask the man's name, but didn't catch the answer; at least she was keeping her head. Then she came upstairs briskly. Canning went ahead into the bedroom, where the tea, now nearly cold, stood on the dressing-table.

"I suppose you heard?"

Canning nodded.

"His name's Weston," she said, as if that were important. "John Weston. You don't *have* to see him, do you?" There was little spirit in her voice, and Canning guessed what she was thinking; she soon confirmed it. "But I suppose if you do, you might find out more about things, George. He'll wait while you dress, I expect."

"Oh, I'd better see him." Canning made the decision for the same reason as he had made most of the others: to prevent Weston—anyone—from wondering why he refused. It was useless to tell himself that no one would dream of the real reason. "I'll shave quickly but won't dress."

"All right. Thank you, George."

It took Canning ten minutes to shave and wash, another five to dab at the scratches, which had started to bleed again. When he combed back his thick, wiry hair, with grey liberally sprinkled among the black, he looked at his strong face which he knew was so deceptive, and wondered what kind of questions the reporter would ask, whether the police knew that he had come here. They possibly didn't.

When he went to the landing, Belle was coming upstairs.

"Shall I bring him up?"

"Yes, when you like."

"I'll bring some more tea and a few biscuits," Belle said, "that will tide you over until he's gone." She didn't prompt him about what to say, but went off quietly, outwardly recovered from the upset which the telephone call had caused.

Canning went into the study. The desk looked as if he had been working all the morning. He put out a new packet of cigarettes, and noticed that several packets had gone from his store. The ashtrays had been emptied and the study dusted; it looked spick and span.

"Here is Mr. Weston," Belle said.

Weston was a stocky, youthful-looking man, probably older than he seemed. He had a good smile, a firm handshake and a casual manner which was probably deceptive. He apologized for disturbing Canning, accepted a cigarette and sat down, with his face turned towards the window; Canning's was in shadow. The light fell on Weston's broad, homely face and on his thinning light brown hair; he wore a well-cut suit of grey Harris tweed.

"Well, now, how do you think I can help you?" Canning asked, and tried to sound brisk.

"I'm after the human interest angle." Weston had a way, rather like Matthew's, of investing everything he said with a cloak of sincerity; and his manner suggested that as one writer to another, they knew just how to approach the subject. "This Pole. I mean. I managed to have a word with him last night, before the police detained him, and he seemed a nice young chap. His wife's so upset that she hardly knows what she's saying, but I gather that he's the kindest man in the world!" Weston smiled. "Of course, they've only been married six months."

"I don't know her." Canning was brisk. "I've only met Waclow once, too."

"Yes, I know—and I also know that you can't tell me what questions you put to him," Weston said, and might have added: "We both know the rules, don't we? and wouldn't dream of breaking them!" "I don't suggest quoting you, but perhaps you could give me an impression or two. Was he aggressive at all, and did he fly off the handle, anything like that?"

"No."

"Took it quietly, then?"

What harm was there in answering that? The quicker he answered the sooner the interview would be over, and Canning would be able to quieten his mind; at the moment, all he could see was the pale, frightened, resigned face of the young Pole.

"You might say he had a kind of dignity."

"Ah, that's what I'm after!" Weston beamed. "He denied it, of course."

"He wasn't charged when I was there."

"Oh, no—that came this morning. But he didn't give you the impression that he knew it was a fair cop, and that he'd lost his chance of getting away with it, did he?"

"I wouldn't say so."

"Did he mention his wife?"

"Only in passing."

"Pity," said Weston. "I'd like to portray them as being desperately worried about each other. No doubt they are, though. I gather from Banfield, who isn't exactly devoted to the Press, that Waclow can't account for his movements on the night of the murder."

"Banfield wasn't satisfied with his story—as you must know."

"Yes. You can't tell me what the story was, I suppose?"

Canning thought: "No, I can't." In his disarming way, Weston was after much more than he pretended, and Banfield would know that the story of the two 'friends' who were to sleep out could only have reached the Press through the interpreter. On the other hand, if the Press helped in the hunt for two men, it would surely give Waclow a chance to find the only two witnesses who might help him. Waclow *had* to be given a chance. True, the money found at his mother-in-law's home made it pretty clear that he had stolen it from the Dales, but he could have done that before leaving for his holiday. Why not start the hunt for the other Poles? If they didn't exist, it would strengthen the case for Bob's innocence of the major crime.

Weston didn't prompt him.

Canning said: "It's a difficult question to decide what I should tell you. I was there as a confidential interpreter, of course. Hasn't Banfield told you anything about Waclow's story?"

"Just said that it was cock-and-bull! You know how it is." Weston shrugged. "Of course he may be right, and

Waclow did do it, but Banfield would want everyone to believe that he's right, anyhow. He—"

"I can't pass that," Canning interrupted. "Banfield wouldn't want the wrong man charged any more than you or I would. I admit that I rather took to Waclow," he added, and managed to smile; it was easier than he had expected, partly because of Weston's easy manner. "You've talked to the Scots wife, apparently."

"She hardly knows what she's saying."

"Didn't she tell you that Waclow met two Poles and spent part of the evening with them?"

"Oh, yes. They're the key to it, are they? Waclow claims that he was with them for the time he was missing, and Banfield gives that tale a raspberry. I suppose you can't blame him. We might run a story asking them to come back, as their compatriot's life might depend on their evidence. And I can make sure that Banfield thinks I got it from Mrs. Waclow. I think I can build up on this all right, you've been very good. Did Waclow say anything about his past?"

"No."

"Plenty of heart-throbs in that, so to speak," Weston told him. "He was captured during the first few days of the attack on Poland, went into a slave labour camp in Germany for most of the war. They found him in one of the smaller concentration camps. Fantastic, that stories like that are almost commonplace, isn't it? Lost all his family—he was only a boy at the time. Fifteen. Things weren't good in Germany when he was released, he couldn't get work, and he couldn't face Poland again under the Russians. He had a pretty rough time for a few years. Then he and the Scots girl met and married, and they came over here. Waclow couldn't do factory work or go down the mines. His health is pretty poor, I gather, he had to work in the open air. He's had a couple of jobs with people who speak German—learning English is proving difficult for him. His earlier jobs were on farms. There was some resentment about employing Polish labour, and he and his wife looked for a private job—he has his permits, of course. I did get one thing out of Banfield," the reporter added, almost as an afterthought.

Canning said: "Did you?" The story twisted the sword of guilt in his own breast. Hadn't Waclow suffered enough? What decent man could let him go on suffering, robbing him of his chance of being free from the ordeal of waiting and of fear, and robbing his wife too, condemning her to days of agony?

"Yes. Nothing known against Waclow in any of the other places. In fact he had good references, everyone seemed to like the chap. I—"

There was a sharp tap at the door. Canning had forgotten that Belle had promised to bring in tea and biscuits. She brought them in on the best silver-plated tray; she always liked to impress the unexpected caller.

"I thought you'd like a cup of tea, Mr. Weston."

"Happy thought." Weston jumped up. "That's very good of you, thanks very much."

Belle put the tray down, poured out a cup, asking the formal questions about tea and sugar in a voice and with a manner which suggested that she hadn't a worry in the world. When she went out, Canning wondered how much she had heard at the door. He wondered if Bob had been listening, too; he couldn't hear anything from the room next door, but might have caught snatches from the landing.

"Did Banfield tell you what evidence he'd got?" He spoke abruptly.

"Not really," Weston said. "I gather it's pretty strong. He wouldn't have risked an arrest otherwise."

"No trace of anyone else at the house that night?"

"He didn't say so." Weston's gaze sharpened. "Have you any ideas?" He certainly wouldn't miss much.

"If it wasn't Waclow, obviously someone else was there," Canning answered.

"Not much argument about that." Weston smiled freely again. "I was hoping you'd got hold of something. In a case like this the police are sometimes too easily satisfied, and some of the boys and I are digging. If we could find that

Waclow wasn't the only visitor it would give Banfield plenty to think about, wouldn't it?" The reporter finished his first cup of tea. "As a matter of fact, Mr. Canning, that's one of the reasons I came to see you. We London newspapermen are strangers down here, and it's a handicap not knowing the district. If you've any suspicion that Banfield might be wrong, or even a soft spot for young Waclow, we'd be very glad of your help. Between you and me, it's already obvious that Waclow wasn't the only one who knew that Jerry Dale often kept a lot of money in the house. There was a gang of youths who hung around the band at rehearsals, and some of them visited the house." Weston took out his own cigarettes and handed the case towards Canning, smiling, casual, while Canning fought to keep his face calm.

14

THE NEW THREAT

CANNING took a cigarette and turned round, pretending to look for his lighter, which was in his dressing-gown pocket. That gave him time to find his composure. When he looked back at Weston, his expression gave nothing away.

"I can't say that I like that idea much. More tea?"

"No, thanks."

"You won't mind if I have some." Pouring out enabled Canning to avoid Weston's eyes again. When he settled back with the cup in his hand, he looked at the newspaperman; and his heart missed a beat. For that split second, it seemed to him that Weston's whole appearance had altered; there was a probing, questioning look in his eyes.

If it had existed, it quickly faded.

"So you don't like the idea," Weston echoed.

"Don't misunderstand me. I've nothing against it in principle." Why the devil should he have, and why say so?

"But it isn't the kind of thing I fancy for myself. I prefer to make my researches at the libraries." Canning forced a smile, and hoped that it looked natural. "No, I won't help you with that. I might as well be definite."

"Much better," Weston agreed. "Perhaps you could suggest someone who would help, though. I thought of Randall of the *Gazette*, but I think he'd regard it as a form of treachery to his lifelong friend the Superintendent."

Canning sipped tea. "He probably would."

"How well do you know Matthew Grant?" asked Weston, and this time the air of nonchalance did not deceive Canning; the reporter almost certainly knew that Matthew lived in this house. "He's hoping to marry your daughter, I gather. *Very* charming girl, if you don't mind me saying so."

"Why should I?" Canning forced another smile. "Matt? I can't see him as a detective."

"He sees himself as one!"

"Oh, does he?" Canning felt as if the pressure were unbearable.

"Perhaps that's exaggerating." Weston decided to have second thoughts. "Jerry Dale is in a pretty bad way, and just can't rest. Matthew Grant seems to think that the best way to help him is to give him something to do."

"Possibly." Canning felt suddenly hot. Until a few moments before, Weston had fooled him, but he wasn't fooled now. The real reason for this visit was coming out; the inquiries about Waclow had been almost incidental. Experienced newspapermen knew where to get the information they wanted. If Weston were seriously thinking of making inquiries about the youths who hung about the band rehearsals, he could get the information from Jerry or any of the members of the band; most would be eager to help. Probably he had found out all he wanted; probably he knew that Bob was one of the 'gang'. He was here to get an impression of his, Canning's, reaction to the probe.

Without dreaming that it might do harm, Celia would tell anyone that the Dale brothers had been helpful to Bob; that

Bob had actually been inside the Marlborough Street house. Weston almost certainly knew that.

The wave of heat subsided; Canning hoped that it hadn't turned his cheeks too red. Weston would miss very little; and if he had come to probe, then he might have told the story of the Pole's unhappy, tormented past so as to work on Canning's nerves. What other reason could there have been for going into such detail?

"So I wondered if you thought Matthew Grant might be a good man to ask for help," Weston went on. "He seems pretty level-headed."

He might mean: "I'm telling you that someone who lives here is going to start investigating, and will soon get round to your son."

Why should it matter so much? Canning asked himself wearily. Why was he almost desperately anxious that the reporter and therefore the police shouldn't find out? He knew that they would, eventually; he was committed to telling them, wasn't he? He had only to say a dozen words now, and the whole miserable business would be over.

But—what about Belle?

"I don't know Matthew well," he said carefully. "I like him. I should say he'd make a good job of anything he attempted. Certainly he feels this business very keenly."

"Exactly my own opinion." Weston stood up, unexpectedly. "You've been very good, and I've taken up more of your time than I meant to. Do thank your wife for the tea, won't you?"

Canning also stood up.

"Yes. I hope I've helped."

Weston shook hands at the head of the stairs, but Canning went down with him. Belle didn't appear, but the drawing-room door was ajar, and Canning thought that he caught a glimpse of Bob. Canning opened the front door, and wind blew in fiercely. Weston walked briskly down the drive, his coat billowing behind him, his stocky figure seeming to carry all before it; he was a man with a purpose.

His car was parked just outside the gates. He didn't turn round or wave, just got in and drove off.

Canning turned; the pressure of the wind made it difficult to close the door.

Bob no longer tried to hide the fact that he was in the drawing-room, and Belle came out of the kitchen. Tension was back in her; it was as if she had some premonition of the nature of the interview.

Bob cried: "What did he want?"

Canning looked at him. That pallor, those brimming eyes, would give him away to anyone who saw it; he was suffering torment. For the second time that morning, Canning felt a twinge of compassion.

"It's inevitable, Bob," he said. "They're spreading their inquiries. What the police don't do, the Press will."

Bob screeched: "But they've arrested someone else, I heard him say so!"

All compassion fled.

Canning felt the urge to turn away, to get out of sight and reach of his son. But he did not. Tight-lipped, he went forward, and Bob retreated into the big room. It was dark, for the lowering clouds were heavier and the wind drove against the windows at the side. Bob backed towards the radio, which seemed his perpetual sanctuary, and he didn't speak. Belle was behind Canning, and she did not interfere; Canning sensed that she was looking at Bob.

"Bob," said Canning very quietly, "would you really stay here, saying nothing, if another man were in danger of being blamed for your crime?"

"I didn't kill him, I tell you, I didn't!" Bob cried.

Could anyone believe him? He shrank back, eyes blazing with terror; they held something else too—hatred. Yes, he hated his father, saw him as the instrument of damnation. Studying him, Canning realized that, and knew that there was no mistake; the realization silenced him.

Belle said abruptly: "Of course he wouldn't."

Bob still kept silent. His lips were parted, there was a little froth at the corners; the trapped animal again, who could be dangerous.

"I hope you're right," Canning said. "You'd better think it over, Bob. It might help you to know that the accused man served in slave labour camps and was put in a concentration camp—at your age. He was rescued, but for years after that he hadn't enough food, and had no home. It's only in the past few months, while he's been in England, that he's known any kind of happiness."

Canning turned on his heel.

It meant leaving Bob and Belle together, but he couldn't bring himself to interfere with them, to tell her to leave the boy to think this over for himself. That would be futile, anyhow; now he knew, if he had ever had the slightest doubt before, that Bob would try to save himself even if it meant letting another man be hanged for the murder.

What would Belle do?

Bob didn't matter; Bob was beyond redemption, he'd known that before. But Belle—

Canning went up to his study. Weston's chair was still drawn up, near the desk. The ends of the two cigarettes that the newspaperman had smoked were in the glass ash-tray near the chair. Canning could picture the man's broad face, his casual manner; and remember the sharpening of his expression, that probing, almost accusing look.

The quicker the authorities got on to Bob, the better; it would take the decision out of his hands, and out of Belle's. But even as he sat there the questions began to burn within him again. His own flesh and blood—how could he turn his back on him?

Hadn't he tried hard enough, couldn't he wash his hands of the boy? Hadn't he the guts to go to Belle now, tell her that it was hopeless, that he was going to telephone Banfield? Could any man argue with himself that it was the wrong thing to do; and was there any reason at all for more delay? Was even the hope of future happiness a justification for doing nothing? Remember the torment in the mind of the Pole, and the misery of his young wife.

Canning went out of the study. The sound of voices floated upstairs. In the bedroom, he dressed slowly. It was nearly a quarter past twelve, and, in spite of everything else, he felt hungry. Belle might have intended to prepare an early lunch, but everything would have been forgotten. He went downstairs; they were still in the drawing-room. He felt an overwhelming desire to hear what they were saying. When he reached the door, only the sound of their voices came through. He touched the handle; if it opened an inch, he could hear, and they were probably too absorbed in what they were saying to notice the handle turning, the door opening.

He opened the door.

Belle was speaking . . .

"And do exactly as I tell you. Do you understand?"

"Yes—yes, Mother."

They were near the end of the talk; Canning couldn't stay any longer. He moved away quickly, went to the kitchen and out into the blustery wind. It wasn't raining, although there was rain in the air. The wind buffeted his face and stung his eyes, but he was glad to have it raging about him, from the moment he had heard the tail-end of the conversation he had felt suffocated. It was less the words than the tone in which they had been uttered. There had been no brusqueness in Belle; nothing to suggest that she had been upbraiding the boy; instead, there had been a conspiratorial air about it, and the "Yes—yes, Mother," hadn't been uttered resentfully but in a curious excited voice, almost as if the boy had seen reason to hope.

Canning went towards the vegetable garden, and glanced behind the garage; his gaze was drawn to it.

The bicycle wasn't there.

Canning stood quite still.

He could see where it had scratched the wood of the garage, and where it had pressed against the beech hedge; that was all. One of them had taken it away. Belle—or Bob?

He turned and looked towards the house. Belle was in the

kitchen, bending over the sink; she looked towards him, and he thought that she smiled. He went into the vegetable garden; there was a toolshed and a small greenhouse; the bicycle might be in either of them. It wasn't. Some evidence had gone; and one of Belle's first thoughts had been to get the bicycle away.

In the revulsion of feeling, he felt sure that she had been fooling him, and that conspiratorial tone was real, not imagined. But could he *be* sure? Even if Belle had tried to soothe the boy's fears she could have done so to try to squeeze some of the bitterness out of him; she might still have hope. She must have recognized the hate in the boy's eyes when Canning had spoken in that tone of loathing.

Rain begain to fall.

Canning went slowly back to the house, dreading the coming encouter; he hadn't said a word to Belle about Weston's inquiries, and she would be full of urgent questions. She was at the gas-stove, lifting a lid off a bubbling pot. Bob wasn't here.

"It's raining, isn't it?" Belle asked briskly. "I didn't think it would hold off for long. Lunch won't be more than twenty minutes or so. You must be famished." In fact, he was no longer hungry. "Bob's laying the table. I think I've persuaded him to repent a little. But I don't know." She turned round, holding a steaming spoon in one hand, the saucepan lid in the other. "I just don't know, George. Sometimes I think he's really evil."

Her look, her shadowed eyes, stemmed his rush of suspicion, switched Canning back to belief in her. He didn't answer, and she turned away. It was several minutes before he could make himself speak.

"Belle."

"Yes."

"Where's the bicycle?"

"What?" She spun round. "It's behind the garage, where you put it."

"It isn't."

She looked dumbfounded, then glanced towards the closed

serving hatch, between the kitchen and the dining-room. She moved towards it, her lips very tightly together.

"He must have taken it away. He was in the garden this morning, said that he had to get some fresh air. I didn't dream that he—"

"We don't need much more telling that he won't make any confession, do we?" Canning asked flatly. He was going to add: "Isn't it time we gave it up, Belle?" but the words wouldn't come; her expression stopped them. She still looked incredulous, and Canning found it almost impossible to believe that she had known about the bicycle; and his fears of a conspiracy weakened.

Belle said: "I'm beginning to be afraid you're right."

"That Pole—"

"I know," Belle said abruptly. "I know how you feel. What else did the reporter have to say?" Now she had turned away from the hatch, was intent on Canning.

He could not bring himself to tell her everything; in his heart he was sure of the real reason for Weston's visit, but it would be difficult to explain; nothing he could quote would make it clear to her. Above everything else, he wanted to make her agree that they should go to Banfield at once. If she knew that the gang of youths was already suspect, she would realize that their cause was hopeless, that no more good could come from prevarication.

"He—and other reporters—aren't sure that Banfield's right. They're making inquiries themselves. So—so is Matthew. Matthew's doing it for Jerry Dale. Sooner or later they're going to find out that other people knew about the money kept at the house."

"That damned fool!" Belle burst out viciously. "I mean Jerry Dale. If he hadn't put temptation in their way, this would never have happened. I hope he realizes it." She began to move about the kitchen, and then opened the oven door; Canning caught a glimpse of roasting meat, heard the fat spitting. She drew out the shelf, turned over the potatoes cooking in the fat, then put everything back quickly. "That won't be long. I'm sorry, George, but I do feel vicious towards Jerry Dale. I suppose one can't blame Matthew for trying to help him." She was still very edgy, sharp-voiced. "Have you thought of the effect of all this on Celia? What she'll feel like when she learns what's happened?"

Canning could only shrug his shoulders.

"We'll just have to break it to her," Belle said wearily. "We can't do anything until we've done that, can we? Is she coming home to-night?"

"She didn't say."

"I'll telephone her at the office this afternoon," Belle said. "It's no use letting it drag on. You can't stand the strain much longer, you look dreadful. They'll start thinking *you* did it, soon." That was a pathetic attempt at being flippant, and it failed grotesquely. "We'd better tell Celia and Matthew to-night, he'll have to know too." She caught her breath. "Do you think it will make any difference to him? In his feeling for Celia, I mean? What will he think when he knows that her brother is a—" she couldn't finish.

"If he's worth anything, it won't make the slightest difference to him," Canning said gruffly. He felt relief creeping over him again; it was as if a heavy weight had been lifted from his shoulders. "You really feel that it can't go on."

"Yes," Belle said tautly. "Yes. I—"

The front-door bell rang.

Every unexpected caller brought tension. This time, it affected Belle worse than Weston's ring. Canning felt his own heart thumping, too. Obviously Belle wasn't in a fit state to answer the bell, so he went. Bob was at the dining-room door, lips parted, eyes reflecting that fear which had become part of him. Canning actually squared his shoulders, and went to the front door as the bell rang again.

He opened it.

" 'Morning, Mr. Canning!" The parcel postman smiled. His little red van was at the gate. "Two for you this morning." They were parcels of books, sent to Canning for review. "We're going to have a proper soaker before the day's out." He was a little weather-beaten man with bright blue eyes. "Nice weather for the ducks, anyway."

"Just right." Canning forced a smile. "Thanks."

"Okay. It's a bit late this morning, three of our chaps are at the police station. Being questioned over this murder case." The murder might have been the only topic in the world. "They do the Marlborough Park district, I suppose the police might think they saw something. Looking for a bike, I'm told," the postman added briskly. "Well, I'd better face it, I suppose, put my oilskins on when I get into the van or I'll catch me death."

A squall of rain struck the side of the house fiercely, and the heavens seemed to open. Rain smashed down and splashed up from the gravel drive and into the porch. The postman drew nearer Canning, who said:

"You'd better wait until it slackens a bit."

"Yes, ta," the postman said, still looking at the rain. "Talk about sheets of it! Bad business, that murder, wasn't it? Must have been the Pole, I suppose, the police don't often make mistakes."

"No." Canning found it impossible to keep back the question which had been thrust into his mind. "What's this about a bicycle?"

The man turned, the shrewd blue eys were close to his; and the postman was earnest.

"One was pinched, last night, and between you and me, Mr. Canning, there was the marks of bicycle tyres on a flower-bed at Mr. Dale's house. Looks as if someone run over the bed in the dark. They'd better hurry up, or the prints will be washed out by this rain, won't they?"

They would be; but that would not handicap the police, who would have made casts of the tyre-marks as soon as they had been found. The police would miss nothing. Canning felt a sense of the remorseless processes of the law. It came to him that the thing that mattered now was to tell Banfield the truth before Banfield found it himself. For the first time, it seriously occurred to him that he and Belle were turning themselves into accessories—this was more than an abstract case of right and wrong. True, the bicycle was gone, but it might be found, and Bob might have left finger-prints on it; Canning himself had almost certainly when he had pushed the machine behind the garage. How long did finger-prints last?

It was now a race between telling Banfield, and Banfield finding out. With the Press working on the gang of youths and the police searching for the bicycle, how could inquiries here be long delayed?

The rain slackened.

"I'll make a dive for it," the postman said. "See you next time." He ran lithely towards his van.

As he did so, a youth appeared, wheeling a bicycle; he came from the shelter of some nearby trees. He wore a trilby hat pulled low over his forehead and a raincoat which looked soaked through. He passed through the gate as the postman met him, but didn't take any notice of the man.

Canning waited at the door.

Belle came from the kitchen. "What was that about a bicycle, George?" She could hardly get the words out.

"There were some tracks at a flower-bed," Canning told her. He knew that Bob, who had come from the dining-room, heard him. He didn't look at the boy. "I wonder who this is." The youth wheeling the bicycle was close to the front door now. In spite of his drenching, he walked with a swagger, and raised a hand in an almost insolent greeting. Before he spoke, he leaned the bicycle against the wall.

He ignored Canning.

"Howdy, Bob," he greeted, and Canning realized that Bob was by his side, Belle just behind him. "I didn't quite hear you on the telephone, I thought I'd come and have a little chat." He grinned; it wasn't a pleasant grin.

Bob seemed petrified.

15

BLACKMAIL

"WELL, you're a fine one," the youth said. "Aren't you going to ask me in?" He stepped on to the porch, and glanced at Canning. "You Bob's old man?"

Canning kept his hands rigid by his sides.

"Cyril, I told you not to—" Bob began squeakily, and then his voice failed him.

"If you want to come in and talk to Robert," Belle said in a surprisingly steady voice, "you can go round to the kitchen, and take your raincoat and things off in there. Go round to the right."

The youth named Cyril looked at her narrowly, then obviously decided that she would stand no nonsense. He gave a mock salute.

"Okay, Ma, I'll keep the carpets clean!" He turned away and started towards the right.

"And take your bicycle to the back," Belle called sharply.

Cyril came back for it. He obviously resented her manner, but was still prepared to do what she told him. He began to whistle as he wheeled the machine away. Bob suddenly raised his hands to his face, and his shoulders began to shake.

Belle looked across him to Canning.

"We don't need telling who that is," she said. "It's the bosom friend of Bob's who knows that he was at the Dales' house." The bitterness in her voice! "Pull yourself together, Bob!"

The boy's shoulders were still bowed.

"George, go and let that lout in, will you?" Belle said. "He'll be at the door by now."

"He can wait a minute. We've got to decide what to do, quickly, Bob!" Canning gripped Bob's right arm and shook it vigorously. "How much does he know? What did you tell him?"

"I can answer that," Belle said quietly. "Bob told me. The little beast doesn't know that you and I have been told, and he wants twenty-five pounds from Bob, to keep him quiet. I know what I'd do with him if I had my way, but—" there was appeal in her eyes, and Canning wasn't sure what it really meant. "We'd better let him see Bob for ten minutes, while we decide what to do. They can go up to Bob's room. This little beast mustn't know that we know, must he?"

"I suppose not," Canning conceded grudgingly.

"Anyone at home?" The visitor called out from the kitchen; he hadn't waited for the door to be opened. His voice was deliberately loud and aggressive, he probably felt that Bob would have to plead with his parents to make the caller welcome. "Smells good, I must say, just my luck to be in time for dinner!"

"Hurry, George," Belle urged, "and don't stand any nonsense from him."

"If I see that lout again in the next five minutes I'll break his neck," Canning growled. "You go and handle him." He took Bob's right arm and led him towards the drawing-room. The kitchen door opened and Cyril appeared, but Belle blocked his view. Canning thrust his son into the lovely room, and closed the door with a bang. Bob staggered against a chair and stood thus, his hands raised in front of his chest and his cheeks smeared with tears.

"Who is that little beast and what does he know?" Canning demanded harshly.

"He—he—he—"

"For God's sake get a hold on yourself!"

Bob gulped and tugged a handkerchief from his pocket. He blew his nose vigorously. In spite of the fresh shock and the way it had fed his fear, hatred for his father showed in his dark eyes.

"He's Cyril—Rigby."

"What does he know?"

"He knows—he knows I stole the bike."

"Does he know why?"

"He—he knows I was going to do a job, I *think* he knows where it was. He wants some money out of me, he says he'll tell the police if I don't pay him twenty-five quid. I've just *got* to get twenty-five pounds!" The shrill voice took on a nervous vigour. "I know Cyril, if he says a thing like that he means it."

"You haven't got twenty-five pounds. If you had, I wouldn't let you give it to him," Canning said. "Let's see if you've any guts at all. Go and talk to him, tell him he can go to the police or go to hell for all you care, but he's not getting a penny out of you."

"But—but he'll—"

"You haven't any choice," Canning growled. "You can't give him the money. You can go down on your knees and beg him to wait, if you feel like it. Or you can tell him to do what he damned well likes. Perhaps you'll realize what good your friends will do you, after this." He turned away, bitterness welling up.

The door opened before he reached it. Belle came in and closed it quietly.

"I've sent your friend up to your room, Robert. You can go and talk to him there for ten minutes." Her eyes were on Canning, questioning; she was asking: "What have you said to him?"

Canning told her.

Bob looked as if he were going to plead with her for the money, but Belle's expression discouraged him. He moved awkwardly towards the door, opened it, and slunk out. Canning went to his wife's side, and stood quite still; then Belle's hand groped for his, and squeezed gently.

"I couldn't stand another day of it," she said. "We're not going to. I suppose we could ask Celia to come home early. I mean, get time off from the office. Now that I've brought my mind to telling the truth. I can't get it over quickly enough. What a fool I've been not to listen to you before." She moved away from him, as if she were afraid of being too sentimental. "I *must* dish up. Dinner will be ruined, and I wanted you to have a really good meal."

In the kitchen, she opend the oven door. The smell of roast beef made Canning realize that he was hungry.

"Roast beef and Yorkshire, baked potatoes and cauliflower a baked jam-roll to follow." Belle took the meat out of the oven; the potatoes were a golden brown, the joint gleamed darkly, perfectly cooked. "Go and make sure that Bob's mixed the mustard and made the horseradish sauce, will you? I doubt if he has."

Canning went out, listened at the foot of the stairs, heard nothing, and then went into the dining-room. Belle's ability to behave calmly in spite of her anguish was quite remarkable and unexpected. This new Belle was a revelation. Even with the two youths upstairs, and Cyril with his foul threats, Canning could still feel a strange buoyancy of spirit when he thought of that.

The mustard and the horseradish sauce were made. He opened the hatch, to tell Belle so.

"Good. We'll be ready in ten minutes, and you can start carving before that. I told Bob to come down at half-past one sharp." It was twenty past. "I suppose we'll have to let the little beast feed with us." Her smile was wan. "I mean the one who's just arrived."

Canning said roughly: "I'm not sitting at the table with him."

Belle closed her eyes, as if she were too weary to continue the fight; but she conquered weariness, and moved towards him.

"Try to, George. It won't be long now. We'll have Celia home as soon as we can—she'll be at lunch now, and we'll telephone immediately we've had ours. When she knows everything, we can make an end of it all. But if you have a row with this dreadful Cyril, he's quite likely to go rushing to the nearest telephone. Try, George."

There was really no choice.

Canning carved the beef, while Belle called up to the youths from the foot of the stairs. She came into the dining-room and served the vegetables.

Canning sat down, wearily; he was still hungry; but for

the guest he would have felt that he could enjoy the meal. He helped himself to horseradish sauce liberally; there was something in its hot, pungent taste which he liked, and which brought out the flavour of the meat. It was a custom to start all together, and he waited.

"You start, George." Belle helped herself to mustard; she didn't like horseradish sauce; nor did Bob. "I'm going to. If they like to let a lovely meal like this get cold, that's their look-out." She maintained outward calmness, and Canning felt his admiration for her strengthening. When she might have been expected to collapse and to be useless, she had shown remarkable self-control. He started to eat. The horseradish was hotter than usual, and his tongue tingled. Yet it brought out the flavour all right.

The door opened and the two youths came in.

Canning knew in a moment that something had happened to restore Bob's self-esteem and build up his nerve. The other lad was as cocky as he had been from the beginning. He wore a pale blue suit; the coat was very square at the shoulders and full in the skirt, a bright red bow tie was crumpled where the rain had trickled between his raincoat and neck. His hair was fair, and brushed straight back from his forehead; his fair eyelashes and eyebrows gave him an almost albino look. His lips were red—lustful, unpleasant. He smirked.

"You sit here," Belle said, and pointed. "Your usual place, Bob."

"Okay, Mum." Bob slid into his seat. He didn't smirk, but he was no longer as craven.

"Horseradish sauce, Cyril?" Belle asked.

"Don't mind if I do," Cyril said. "Ta."

He ate with his elbows sticking out, and when he was masticating, held the knife and fork pointed towards the ceiling; he wasn't exactly a silent eater, either. Canning felt that he couldn't sit at the table with him any longer, or he would explode. Belle's silent pleading kept him where he was.

Canning didn't exactly enjoy the meal. The taste of the

horseradish lingered much more than usual, his tongue burned, and the roof of his mouth felt very dry. He drank plenty of water. Cyril kept up a running fire of comment on this, that and the other thing, most about racing, football pools and television. He did not mention the murder. Bob ate heartily; he seemed better now than he had been from the moment he had thrown stones at the window. Canning felt desperately anxious to find out why, but he kept silent.

Belle went out to dish up the baked jam-roll. Canning's tongue and mouth burned. He drank more water, wishing that he hadn't had so much sauce. He had never known the pungent bite of horseradish to last for so long. But the roll, beautifully cooked and with short pastry which melted in the mouth, made him forget that for a few moments. He finished eating before the others. Not once had Cyril Rigby addressed a remark directly to him; that at least saved him from refusing to answer.

His throat began to hurt.

He got up, said: "I'll be in the drawing-room," and went out. His anxiety to find out what plot the two youths had hatched was offset by his own discomfort. It soon became pain. He forgot the furious anger he felt towards Cyril, forgot that he was to ring Celia and try to get her back before the usual time. Telling her and telling the police no longer mattered. His throat was really painful; it seemed to be closing up; he couldn't swallow well but kept trying to; it didn't help. The roof of his mouth and his tongue seemed as if they had pins and needles. Suddenly pain gripped his stomach, and for a moment he was rigid in agony. The pain eased slightly, but didn't go altogether.

He forced himself to get out of his chair and moved towards the door.

"Belle," he called. "Belle." He could hardly hear his own words. Another pain stabbed through his stomach, and suddenly he felt sick. He fought against that. He was near the door, but couldn't move easily, his legs had grown numb and wouldn't carry him. He shuffled forward, then almost doubled up with another fiery pain in his stomach; and the sickness threatened again.

"Belle," he croaked.

The door remained closed. Making a great effort, he reached it; but there was no strength in his fingers, he couldn't grip the handle. Now pain all merged together; in his throat, his mouth, his arms and legs, but worse of all those piercing swords which cut his vitals.

There was singing in his ears, yet numbness too. He tried to turn the handle of the door but failed, and leaned against it. He had to get out, had to get to the cloakroom, the sink, anywhere. He retched.

"Be—Be—Belle."

He couldn't get the words out, because the pain and tightness at his throat were so bad. He had no moment free from pains, but none was worse than those which tore at his mind when the truth sprang into it.

He had been poisoned.

16

NIGHTMARE

CANNING felt something move against him, but did not know what it was. He leaned against the door, bending low to try to ease the agony in his stomach, but nothing made any difference; and the horror of full realization was added. The movement came again, and he heard a voice but wasn't sure whose it was because of the numbness of his ears. He had to move away from the door; staggered; and would have fallen but for a chair. He clung to it.

"George!"

It was Belle. She appeared in the doorway, undoubtedly Belle but moving oddly, jerkily, with a big face, very wide shouldered, a blurred Belle. She reached him and he felt her arms and leaned against her.

"Gerra—gerra—gerra—" he tried to articulate; wanted desperately to tell her to get a doctor. "Gerra—do—do—"

"*Robert!*" cried Belle. "*Robert!*" She began to help Canning towards the hall. Then Bob appeared. "Help me upstairs with your father." Canning knew that was what she said, although the words seemed indistinct, as if she had also been affected by the same constrictions in her throat. Bob had a broad, grinning, blurred face; a *grinning* face. He was all teeth. Bob; the devil he'd sired, Bob hated him. "*Help me with him!*" screamed Belle.

Bob came to his side. Canning staggered across the hall but knew that he would never be able to get up the stairs. Then he forced his tortured limbs to move, heading for the door of the little cloakroom. Belle realized what he was doing, let him go and pushed the door open. He staggered inside. He was violently sick, but that did not ease the pains; they became worse, awful, terrible. He felt himself fainting, just couldn't bear the pain.

Bob—hatred—murder—poison. His only thoughts were in single words. Bob—hatred—murder—poison. He heard voices, but didn't know what was being said. He twisted himself round and then collapsed on to a small stool against the cloakroom wall. He clutched at his stomach but there was no strength in his hands or arms. He knew that he was groaning, a wheezy kind of groan because he could not get his breath properly.

There were faces. Belle's, Bob's, Cyril's. He could no longer tell one from another, couldn't be sure that anyone was grinning, but he could remember Bob's teeth and the grin.

Hatred—poison.

He felt that he couldn't breathe at all; the constriction at his throat was so great. He laboured for breath and that brought more pain. Oh, God, stop it, stop it, give him some rest, give him some rest. He was cold, frozen; he was burning with pain. Oh, God, help him, help him.

He did not see Belle at the telephone, Bob standing watching her, Cyril Rigby leaning against the wall near the dining-room, with his face twisted in pain. He did not hear Belle beating at the telephone as if panic-stricken, or see Bob take out a cigarette and light it with trembling fingers. He did not hear Cyril groan, making Bob look sharply towards him.

"Why don't they answer?" Belle cried shrilly. She banged the platform up and down. "Why don't they—" she broke off, catching sight of Cyril, his face white, his eyes glassy with pain.

Canning retched again in the cloakroom.

"Cyril's ill too," Bob muttered. "What—what's the matter with the telephone?"

"The fools won't answer, They—"

There was a ring at the front-door bell. None of them had heard footsteps. Belle straightened up, still holding the telephone. Bob's lips dropped open and he stared at the door. Cyril Rigby began to breathe in a strange, whistling way, and his face was convulsed.

"Who—" began Bob.

"*See who it is, you idiot!*" Belle screeched.

Bob went slowly towards the door, as if he were also affected by the paralysis which had gripped his father. His fingers fumbled at the knob, it was some time before the door opened.

"What's happening here?" a man demanded.

It was eldery Dr. Hall, purposeful and vigorous. He stepped across the threshold, pushing past Bob. He heard Canning and saw Cyril, glanced at Belle and said sharply:

"What is it, what's caused all this?"

Belle dropped the telephone; it didn't fall into the cradle but hung on its cord, nearly touching the floor.

"Oh, thank God it's you! I don't know, they were taken ill after dinner. My husband is—"

Canning screamed.

Hall was suddenly a man of great authority, not gruff, not vaguely absent-minded.

"Robert, go and get the case at the back of my car. The small black case. Hurry. *Run.*" He gave Bob a push. "Mrs. Canning, tell me just when it started. Quickly."

"Just after lunch, half an hour—*less* than half an hour ago.

He—my husband went into the drawing-room. I thought he was resting. I heard a—a peculiar noise, and hurried to see what it was. He—he couldn't speak properly, he was in such pain. He could hardly move. Oh, what's happening to him, what's happening?"

The sounds from the cloakroom were frightening; a convulsive gasping, groaning sound. Hall stepped in and looked at Canning, turned round and said clearly:

"Go next door, see if the telephone is working there. Call the police and have them send and ambulance. *At once.*" He barked, as Belle stood without moving. "At once." She turned towards the door. "And tell your son to hurry with my case." He did not wait for her to but stepped to Cyril Rigby's side. Rigby was sliding down the wall, crouched up as if the cramping pains in his stomach were too much for him to bear. His eyes were opening and closing, his lips working; suddenly his whole body went into convulsions.

"Is—is this it?" It was Bob, with the black case.

"Yes. Take his coat off, roll up his sleeve." Hall motioned to Cyril, then put the case on the telephone table and opened it. His movements were quick but precise, and soon he was breaking the top of a small capsule, putting a hypodermic needle into it. He filled the syringe, slowly, then changed the needle, all very swiftly. Bob was struggling to get Cyril's coat off, Cyril was making inarticulate noises; the fit of convulsions had passed.

Dr. Hall went into the cloakroom. Canning was crouching over the hand-basin, struggling for breath. The doctor put the syringe carefully on the glass shelf above the basin and slipped Canning's right arm out of his sleeve; that was done while Bob was still struggling with his task. Hall pushed up Canning's shirt sleeve, then plunged the needle in, pressing the plunger slowly. Canning gave a sudden, convulsive start, jerked his arm, and the needle broke.

"Damn!" exclaimed Dr. Hall. He looked at the cylinder; most of the liquid had gone. "I don't think I've any more strychnine," he said to himself. "Did I put that digitalin in? I've no atropine, I know." He left Canning and hurried to his open case. "Digitalin, digitalin." He picked up a capsule, peered at it. "Ah, yes." He filled the syringe again, fitted another needle; and although there seemed to be a hundred little movements necessary, he finished quickly. He turned to Cyril. Bob had the coat off, but hadn't rolled up the sleeve. "Roll his sleeve up!" Hall bellowed, and Bob sprang forward. Cyril was sitting on the floor, his legs twisted, his face working. "Hold his arm." Bob took Cyril's wrist. "Keep it still, you fool!" Dr. Hall plunged the second needle in, and pumped slowly. Bob couldn't keep the arm from jerking, but the needle didn't break. "All right, that'll do. Go and see if your mother's found a telephone. Damned storm."

Outside, the wind was howling, the branches of the trees were bending.

Bob went out; the door slammed after him.

"Must get them to hospital," Dr. Hall said, in a studiously calm voice. He went in to see Canning, dragged him away from the basin and sat him on the W.C. Then he tried to get the point of the needle out, but failed.

"Can't do anything more for them here." Hall stood quite still, with a groaning man on either side of him, and Rigby's convulsions seemed to get worse. "I wonder, I wonder." He walked into the dining-room. The meat and vegetables had been cleared off but the condiments were still on the table. "I wonder," he repeated, and looked at the horseradish sauce; it had a pinkish tinge. "Yes, I would say so, I would say so." He touched the sauce with his forefinger and tasted it cautiously, looking towards the ceiling, as if invoking aid. "*Very* little doubt," he said. He went out of the dining-room, found the kitchen and looked in the larder; on a shelf were several empty jam jars and some glass pots, one of them with a screw cap. He took this, washed it out under a tap, washed a spoon and went back into the dining-room. "Monkshood," he said to himself, and filled the sauce into the jar, screwed on the cap and put the jar into his pocket. It made a bulge.

Cyril was making less noise, and not squirming so much.

The only sound from the cloakroom was of Canning's gasping breathing.

Dr. Hall went back into the kitchen. There was a lot of refuse in a garbage bin beneath the sink. He pulled it out and poked through it, wrinkling his nose. He found a small piece of green with the top of a root attached like a small stunted parsnip. He looked at the pinkish colour that smeared the surface where it had been cut.

"*Very* little doubt," he repeated, and pocketed this. Then he heard someone calling, and hurried into the hall.

Belle Canning and her son were coming in.

"Did you get the police?"

"Yes," Belle gasped. "They're sending an ambulance at once." She turned towards the cloakroom. "How is he? What's happened to him?" She neither looked at nor seemed to think of Cyril. "Oh, George, George."

"There's nothing else we can do until the ambulance gets here—it won't take long, we won't save much time, if any, if we try to get them into cars."

"He'll recover, won't he? He looked terrible but you'll save him," Belle twisted round and gripped the doctor's arms. "Tell me you'll save him!" Her face was distorted, the lips turned back over her even teeth; she was shivering.

"I'll do everything I can," Dr. Hall said in a sharp voice. "Let me go, at once." Belle snatched her hands away. "What did they eat that you didn't, Mrs. Canning?"

"We all had the same, everything," She hardly knew what she was saying. Bob stood in the hall, gulping. "Everything, and he enjoyed—"

"The sauce—did you have the horseradish sauce?"

She raised her arms and her eyes rounded, became huge and glittering.

"No!"

Dr. Hall turned to Bob. "Did you?"

"Why—I—no."

"All right," Dr. Hall said. "You'll both be all right. Now, Mrs. Canning, get some hot-water bottles at once, and then bring some blankets. Quickly please." He turned to the boy. "Robert, I want you to help me with your father. We'll lay him down on the floor. Come along."

Canning was breathing with a series of gasping noises. His eyes opened and closed, twitching; his lips wouldn't keep still, Dr. Hall did most of the work, Bob seemed to be in a daze. "All right, now go and get two cushions," Dr. Hall ordered. He went to Cyril and straightened the youth out. Cyril was exactly the same as Canning, but his movements were less violent. "I'll be lucky if I get them to the hospital alive," Dr. Hall muttered. "This will teach me always to have a stomach pump in the car." He stared in vexation at the door, which shook under a gust of wind. "Why *don't* we learn?" He fumbled in his pocket for cigarettes, and had to push the pot aside. "Peculiar," he said *sotto voce*. "Don't they *know*?"

Belle arrived, with blankets. She had overcome the storm of hysteria, was very pale and bright-eyed but fairly composed.

"The bottles won't be long, doctor." She spread a blanket over Canning. She didn't ask again whether he would live, but turned and, with a completely detached air, put another blanket over Cyril; then a second over her husband. She stood looking down at Canning's strong face.

"What the devil's keeping that boy!" Dr. Hall ejaculated suddenly. He glared at the drawing-room door. Bob appeared, with a cushion under each arm, looking stupid. Belle went off to the kitchen.

"Will they—will they *die*?" Bob asked in a cracked voice.

"I'll do everything I can," Dr. Hall said gruffly. "Put one of those under that man's head." He pointed to Cyril, and pushed the other cushion under Canning's head. Then he took out a gold hunter watch and smoothed the face with his thumb. It was nearly a quarter to three. "Say ten minutes. It's quite ridiculous that there isn't an ambulance in Lingham. Something ought to be done about it." He heard Belle behind him. "Ah, that's right, Mrs. Canning. Must keep them warm." She carried two bottles, and put one beneath the blankets covering Canning. "Now there's nothing else we can do until the ambulance arrives. I think you had better come and sit down." He led the way into the drawing-room.

"I shall stay here," Belle didn't move after him.

Dr. Hall shrugged and pulled a chair into the hall, made her sit down, then watched the way she stared at Canning's twisted features. Men in convulsions looked ugly, unrecognizable. Canning was far more violent than Cyril Rigby, who was only twitching occasionally. Dr. Hall went across and looked at him; his face had a bluish tinge.

The old man shook his head, very slowly, and glanced at his watch again. Five minutes had passed.

Then two women arrived, from next door; Belle stirred herself. The ordinary formal things were said in hushed voices, before everyone fell silent. Dr. Hall looked at his watch. "I'll soon wish I'd used cars. Er—had to call at the end of the road, thought I'd have a look at your son, Mrs. Canning. Lucky I did. I—ah!" He heard a motor outside, and hurried to open the front door. It wasn't the ambulance, but a police patrol car. The police often came to the scene of an emergency call for an ambulance. "It's the police," he said, "the ambulance won't be long, now."

By chance, he glanced at young Canning's face. He saw such fear in those dark eyes that he could not move, could only stand and stare. Then he looked at Mrs. Canning, who had turned away from her husband and watched her son; Dr. Hall could not understand the look in her eyes. He only knew that this was a very bad business, very bad indeed; and that he ought to have a word with the police quickly.

He went to meet the two uniformed officers who were coming up the drive. As he reached them, the ambulance appeared down the rough road.

17

MATTHEW

MATTHEW GRANT sat at his desk in an office overlooking Minchester High Street, the *Gazette* offices, and some of the timbered and thatched buildings which gave the town its charm. He could just see the spire of the cathedral, seven hundred years old; and, if he moved his chair a little, he could see the hospital, on a hill just outside the town. The rain stopped and the wind dropped. He was not thinking of the hospital, the cathedral or the weather.

This was the first time he had really been alone since leaving the Cannings' house with Celia, when he had learned about Peter's murder. That had become one of the accepted things, yet was still difficult to believe; it was hard to imagine that he would never be able to look across the street and see Peter walking into the *Gazette* offices. Peter had handled all the publicity for the Jerry Dale Band; as often as not, when he had finished at the *Gazette*, he would stroll across to this office. Usually he timed the call to coincide with morning tea, or for a quick one at the old *George & Dragon* which was a few doors along.

John Weston, the man from the *Clarion*, came out of the *Gazette* building. Watching him, Matthew knew that his spell of solitude was nearly over. He liked the chap. Other Fleet Street men he had met in the last twenty-four hours hadn't really registered, but Weston stood out as a character in his quiet unassuming way, with a quick mind and something more. Matthew recognized it as a rare thing; a quality of goodness. He knew that he might be exaggerating, but it struck him that way. Weston was probing deeply, even though the police did not approve and Banfield had twice been surly to the point of rudeness. Weston was simply not satisfied that Waclow the Pole had killed Peter. Everyone else had seemed to be.

Weston had telephoned half an hour before, to say that he would be looking in, about half-past four. It was now five past.

If Celia, in the office above, were looking out of her window, she would see exactly the same scene, except that she would see more of the cathedral and the hospital. Matthew smiled, amused by his own mellowing whenever he thought of her. She eased all tensions, had a soothing influence; the very sight of her did something to him.

He had spent an hour here, dictating urgent letters. His secretary would soon bring them in for signature. His drawing board was covered over with a large sheet of brown paper, to keep the dust off some plans he had been drawing up for a new hospital wing.

His secretary tapped and opened the door.

"It's Mr. Weston, sir."

"Show him in, Flo, and bring us some tea."

"Yes, sir."

Matthew was standing up when Weston came in. Weston was on the short side, and burly; if he ever ran to fat he would become a tub of a man. He had a faint likeness to George Canning, in expression rather than feature; the same kind of grey eyes. He smiled.

"Just in time for tea," Matthew said.

"Quite by accident!" Weston dropped into a proffered chair and took out cigarettes. They lit up.

Matthew, watching the newspaperman closely, decided that there was something on his mind, and that it probably meant he had made some progress. He had been making inquiries among a group of youths who had hung about Jerry and Peter Dale at rehearsals, which they always held in a room at the Town Hall, *the* venue in Minchester for dances. He already knew that Bob Canning had been one of them. Matthew began to think that Weston had something disquieting to say; he felt a twinge of apprehension but it didn't affect his outward appearance.

"Solved everything, Weston?"

"No. I've acquired another puzzle," Weston was pulling

very hard at his cigarette. "It will be a nasty shock for you, I'm afraid. And for Miss Canning."

Matthew didn't speak, but apprehension turned into alarm.

"Her father's been taken seriously ill," Weston said quietly. "He's at the hospital. It's touch and go."

Matthew said blankly: "George Canning? But he was as fit as—" he broke off. That wasn't true, Canning hadn't looked so good yesterday morning, Celia had been worried; she came near to worshipping her father. "Does Celia know?"

"I shouldn't think so."

"I'll go up—" Matthew sprang to his feet.

"Wait a bit," Weston advised, and there was a touch of authority in his voice, more than a hint that Matthew hadn't heard the worst. "I had a word with the commissionaire downstairs, he'll ring you if the police should arrive. I don't think they will yet."

Matthew had his back to the window. In shadow, his face looked very strained. He said nothing, but his expression asked the question: "Why the police?"

"Canning was poisoned," Weston said.

Matthew didn't move. "I don't get it." His voice went rather high.

"It happened at lunch-time. I don't know the full story but it's aconite poisoning. There were two victims—a friend of Miss Canning's brother, Cyril Rigby, was the other. He died before they got him to hospital, but Canning's putting up a fight. I hate to say this, Grant, but I've been looking for Rigby. I've reason to think that he knows more than he should about Peter Dale's murder. And he was at the Cannings' House. Of course it may be a coincidence, but—" Weston didn't finish.

There was a tap at the door; neither called out. The tap came again. Matthew looked towards the door sharply.

"What is it?"

"The tea, sir."

"Oh, yes. Bring it in, Flo." The door opened and the

girl glanced at them uncertainly as she put two cups of tea on Matthew's desk.

"One with, one without," she said, "the one with the spoon's got the sugar in."

"Thanks." Matthew made it obvious that he wanted her to get out quickly. She was a slim, lank-haired, unobtrusive girl. She looked back quickly from the door, as if the expression on Matthew's face puzzled her.

Matthew passed the tea with the spoon to Weston.

"First things first," he said. "When did you last hear from the hospital?"

"Ten minutes ago. Randall telephoned while I was in his office. He's very cut up. A lot of Minchester people have a high opinion of your prospective father-in-law."

"So they should," Matthew said emphatically. "Some also think he's woolly-headed and hasn't a commercial sense, but—no, first things first. What did the hospital say?"

"I've told you. He's fighting."

"They aren't hopeful?" What would Celia say? Feel?

"Aconite poisoning is often fatal."

"Aconite poisoning," Matthew echoed. He thought that over. "Can you tell me anything about that?" He was obviously trying to concentrate but had something else on his mind; Celia. He could picture her working in the office above.

"Aconite comes from monkshood," Weston told him. "That's a fairly common wild-flower. Rather like horseradish. I was lucky. The news knocked Randall over so completely that he talked more than he usually does—that is, he said more that matters! He'd been to the hospital and had a talk with Dr. Hall, the family doctor. Hall is pretty sure that it's aconite poisoning. He'd brought away the horseradish sauce that—"

"Horseradish sauce. George Canning goes for that whenever he has a chance," Matthew said slowly. He was beginning to ache, for Celia. "Do you mean that this stuff was in the sauce?"

"It could have been and it looks that way, although I

shouldn't take it for granted yet. Apparently Dr. Hall looked in by chance, he was close by and had promised to see Bob Canning again. If he'd been half an hour later there probably wouldn't have been a chance. Banfield's out at the house now."

Matthew said: "This gets worse." For Celia, it would be horror.

"That's why I don't expect him to worry Miss Canning just yet," Weston said. "I'm hellish sorry about this, Grant. One thing after another. The trouble is—" he broke off, and picked up his tea, drank it quietly and put the cup down noisily in the saucer. "Miss Canning's my great worry. I almost wish I hadn't been sent down here. Not often I come across a couple like you and Miss Canning whom I take to so quickly." His smile was taut. "And I've been the means of piling up trouble for her."

Matthew just looked at him.

"Some of her brother's friends cracked wide open," Weston said. "I've told Banfield. There was a lot of loose talk about breaking in on the Dales because of the money that's often tucked away in there. One of them says that Bob Canning and a crony, Cyril Rigby, got into a huddle and made plans. They stole a bicycle—one of them did, anyhow. The stolen bicycle was used at the Dales' house—there were tyre-tracks in the yard it was stolen from which matched those in the flower-bed. You know all about that. There's a hunt on for it, now." He paused, but obviously hadn't finished. "I found out something else which I almost wish I hadn't."

Matthew said gruffly: "Pile it on."

"On the night—well, early morning—of the murder Bob Canning was seen cycling up the road leading to your house. A neighbour was up at five to catch the early train, and was at his gate waiting for a taxi, which arrived soon afterwards. He says he recognized Bob. This morning, about nine o'clock, Bob was seen by a hedger who'd been clearing out some ditches, pushing a bicycle towards the quarry not far from the house. Banfield's sent men out to look for it, I don't know whether it's been found yet. But by the time you add all these things together, it makes a pretty weighty total, doesn't it?"

"He'd had a fight," Matthew said, as if speaking to himself. "He'd a cut on his cheek and his shoulder was badly twisted. Celia was worried about it. He's not exactly following in his father's footsteps."

"I don't know how much you know about Master Robert Canning," Weston said quietly, "but I can tell you that he has a foul reputation in Minchester. He's been sacked for thieving from two places, and only saved from prosecution by his father's influence. Or rather, because the people concerned didn't want to distress George Canning any more than they had to. He's a vicious young man, Grant, and the police have been keeping an eye on him. Banfield's worried about the whole business because he respects George Canning so much."

"Where did you learn all this?" Matthew was abrupt. He moved away from the window, the tea untouched on his desk. A cigarette, unlit, was between his lips.

"Round and about. The trouble at *Hillview* really made Randall open up," Weston told him. "Nearly everyone who knows him has prophesied a bad end for Bob Canning."

"Do you know," Matthew said very softly, "this is scaring me." He was near the door. "I must go and see Celia. You won't—" he checked himself, and forced a smile. "Of course you won't tell her all this. Not that she needs much telling about her brother, he's a family nightmare."

"A family with two nightmares," Weston said deliberately.

"What the devil do you mean?"

"The wife gives Canning a hell of a time."

Matthew's voice was very low. "You certainly get around, don't you? Where did you learn that?"

"It's common knowledge," Weston said. "The impression in Lingham and in parts of Minchester is that she's a bitch, and Canning ought to have left her years ago. Miss Canning certainly knows that, she even hinted at it last night. You couldn't have missed that. And I gather that Canning tried to keep a hold on Bob, and Mrs. Canning prised it loose whenever he did get a grip. Matt Grant, I don't like the situation a bit."

"Like it!" Matthew hadn't any colour left. "Think it's any use trying the hospital again?"

"No. It'll be several hours before they can say whether they'll pull Canning round. They won't be certain, then, but if he gets through the next six hours, I gather that he'll have a good chance." Weston stood up. "The police are in possession at the house, of course. The last I heard, Mrs. Canning and Bob were still there." He saw Matthew pressing his thumb against his forehead. "The thing you and Miss Canning are going to have to accept, Grant, is that aconite doesn't get into horseradish sauce by accident very easily."

Matthew didn't speak, but went out of the office. His secretary glanced up from her typewriter, started to speak, but stopped. He went on to the landing outside the office, and up to the next floor. By the glass doors which led into the offices of the firm of solicitors where Celia worked, he stopped to press his thumb against his forehead again, and moved it round and round, as if to relieve a sharp pain. He knew that he must look badly upset. Celia would be alarmed the moment she saw him. He went in, and saw one of the partners of the firm, a middle-aged, unctuous man.

"Hallo, Grant."

"Hallo, Pendle." Matthew's forehead was shiny, and Pendle looked at him curiously. "I wonder if Celia can leave at once? I've some very bad news for her. Her father's —seriously ill."

"My dear fellow, I *am* sorry. Yes, of course. I'll send for her at once." Pendle snapped his fingers at an office boy, who came hurrying. "Ask Miss Canning to come here, Sutton." He stood ill-at-ease, staring into Matthew's face. "It's not *too* bad, I hope."

"Grim," Matthew said. "You're very good." He didn't think much of himself because he was going to scare Celia, but he hadn't time to pull himself together, and this had to be done quickly. He watched the door through which the office boy had gone, and saw Celia coming along quite composed until she saw him. Then she missed a step, and approached more slowly.

"Thanks," Matthew said mechanically to Pendle. He took Celia's arm, and didn't try to force a smile. They went out; the landing was empty. "Sorry, darling," he said. "It's knocked me over."

Celia said very quietly: "What is it, Matt? Have they—have they arrested Bob?"

18

HELD FOR QUESTIONING

MATTHEW, with his hand on Celia's arm, felt a shock of surprise, as she asked that so quietly. The candour of her blue eyes had never shone more clearly. She wasn't acutely distressed at the possibility, and had jumped to it in a way which astonished him.

"They—no. Why do you think they might?"

"I haven't been happy about it since I heard what had happened," Celia told him. "I knew there was something badly wrong. Bob sneaking home when he did, and hurt—and Mother and Father behaving so oddly. I didn't fully realize it until I got to the office, because Peter's death shocked me. Then I began to wonder if—but you say that's *not* it."

"Let's go down to my office." They started down. "Darling, your father's seriously ill."

He felt her body stiffen, and she stopped. He made her go on, and told her slowly, trying to soften the news. By the time they reached the office Celia knew practically everything. She nodded to Weston, who had taken Matthew's place at the window. Except for chalk-white cheeks, she looked more collected than Matthew.

"Can I go and see Dad?"

"Not a hope," Weston said.

"I must go to Mother at once."

"I'll drive you home." Matthew picked up a cigarette, hardly thinking about what he was doing. "Weston, will you telephone Jerry Dale and tell him I can't come round as promised?"

"Of course."

"Thanks."

"My bag's upstairs," Celia said. But she didn't move yet. "Mr. Weston, what do you really think about this?"

"I don't know what to think."

"*Was* it an accident?"

"It could have been."

"I see," Celia turned towards the door. "Let's go, Matt." They linked arms as they went out, and Matthew forgot to tell his secretary that he would not be back. Yet he felt less keyed-up because Celia had taken it so well. He should have known that she would. He didn't go up to her office with her, but waited at the head of the stone stairs. He could just see the hall and the bright daylight coming in at the main entrance. He could hear cars passing, and the rumble of a bus. Then shadows appeared on the hall floor; next, big brown shoes, and brown trousers.

"I'm ready," Celia said, from behind him.

"Good." They started down the stairs, but hadn't gone far before two men appeared in front of them; Banfield and a police sergeant.

All four stopped.

Banfield's face looked ruddier than ever, his eyes seemed small, his little mouth was set very tightly. Apparently he didn't like the job he was coming on. He looked intently at Celia, then relaxed, as if guessing that she already knew something.

"Ah, Miss Canning. I was just—"

"How is my father?" she asked abruptly.

"He's—well, he's very ill. I'm sorry." Banfield spoke awkwardly, and gave the impression that he was out of his depth. Matthew thought that he was feeling the pull of sentiment, because personal friendship was being dragged into the orbit of his daily work. "I wonder if you can spare me a few minutes."

"Let's go up to my office," Matthew suggested.

"Thank you, yes."

Weston was coming out. Banfield gave him a sour look, further evidence that he had no love for the Fleet Street man. Where most would have lingered, Weston said briefly:

"I've 'phoned Jerry Dale. Good evening, Superintendent." He ran downstairs.

Lanky Flo was at the typewriter. She swung round when the party entered, and started to get up.

"You carry on," Matthew said, and opened the door of his office. Celia went in, Banfield followed, the detective sergeant waited for him. Banfield coughed. Matthew said: "Sit down, darling," but Celia turned to look at Banfield and didn't seem to hear the words.

"I have to ask you a few questions," Banfield said, articulating very carefully. "Obviously you know what's been happening." He probably didn't realize how much she knew. "I should tell you that I've found it necessary to bring your mother and your brother into Minchester for questioning."

Celia groped behind her, as if for a chair. Matthew helped her to sit down. The only one of the four who seemed completely free from emotion was the sergeant, who stood with his back to the door, and took a shorthand notebook and a pencil out of his pocket.

"When were you last at your home, *Hillview*?" Banfield asked.

"Yesterday morning."

"You haven't been back since?"

"No."

"Were the other members of your family on good terms with one another?" Banfield asked.

Matthew thought: "The clumsy brute!" but he didn't

speak. What else could Banfield ask? Wasn't it better for him to get to the point as quickly as he could?

Celia said: "As far as I know, everything was quite normal."

"All three were at home, were they?"

"I only saw my father. He told me—" Whatever she was thinking or feeling, Celia answered clearly, candidly. Banfield made it clear that he knew about Bob's early hours homecoming, that he wanted to find out if there had been any unusual stresses and strains at the house. If she had set out to be non-committal, Celia could not have succeeded better.

Banfield seemed to expect nothing more; the sergeant made his notes freely.

"Did your father always have horseradish sauce with roast beef, Miss Canning?"

"If he could get it."

"Was the supply usually bought from the grocer's or was it home-made?"

"Home-made."

"The plant was grown in the garden, perhaps."

"Yes."

"Do you know what monkshood is, Miss Canning?"

Celia closed her eyes, as if she not only knew what the plant was but understood the significance of the question.

"Yes."

"Would you recognize the root of monkshood, as distinct from horseradish?"

"I—I don't know. I would know—" she paused for the first time. In the pause the telephone bell rang. Banfield looked at it testily, Matthew leaned across the desk and lifted the receiver. Celia looked at him, perhaps glad of a chance to think, to postpone answering the questions.

"Hallo?"

"Grant, don't let Banfield know I'm calling," a man said. "This is Weston. I don't know what Banfield's after but he'll probably try to make Miss Canning talk while she's off her balance. If you think his questions get too sharp, advise her to ask for legal advice. She doesn't have to answer questions at this stage. Banfield's a wily old bird, don't let him fool you. Understood?"

"Yes," Matthew said. "Yes, thanks. Good-bye." He rang off at once. Banfield looked questioningly, as if he sensed that the call had something to do with his presence. "Sorry," Matthew went on. "You know, you look all in, Celia."

She didn't answer.

"I won't keep Miss Canning much longer," Banfield promised quickly; there was a hostile gleam in his eyes. "This monkshood and horseradish similarity," he went on heavily. "You aren't sure that you would be able to tell them apart?"

"No."

"What else were you going to say?"

Celia hesitated, glanced at Matthew as if for moral support, and said very quietly: "Why are you asking me all these questions, Superintendent?"

"Your answers may help in the inquiries."

"Miss Canning is—" began Matthew.

"Leave this to me, please." Banfield became almost aggressive. "Mr. Canning is dangerously ill, from poisoning. I have to find out how the poison was administered."

"I don't think I want to say anything else," Celia told him, in a quiet, determined voice. "I'd like to see my mother, Superintendent. May I?"

"Very soon, I hope. Miss Canning—"

"Let's call it a day," Matthew said abruptly. "Celia needs a rest, it's been a hell of a shock. You don't have to answer his questions, darling."

Banfield looked at Celia, made no protest, just said with quiet emphasis:

"Your father has been poisoned, Miss Canning. It may have been accidental. It is also possible that it was self-administered and—there is no point in beating about the bush—it could have been given to him by someone else. If you can answer my questions at this stage it may save a lot of time later, and it could also save you and others a great deal of distress. *Would* your father know the difference between monkshood and horseradish?"

Celia said: "Yes," She was quiely emphatic.

"How can you be sure?"

"He—he once showed me."

"When?"

"In the autumn. He'd dug up the horseradish and was storing the roots in sand. One or two monkshood roots had become mixed with—the others." Celia's eyes were becoming glassy, as if her head ached unbearably. "He's a keen gardener, and had noticed the difference. He—he cut one of the monkshood roots."

"What happened?"

"One changed colour, and was tinged pink. The other stayed white."

"Where were you, when your father demonstrated this?"

"In the garden shed."

"Just you and your father?"

Celia closed her eyes again.

"I think we've had enough," Matthew said firmly.

Banfield snapped: "Mr. Grant, be good enough—" He broke off, and they glared at each other, while the sergeant stopped making notes and Celia sat very still, looking from one man to the other.

"It's all right, Matt," she said at last. "I'll answer anything he wants to know, if I can. If it will help to find out the truth—" she caught her breath.

"You're very sensible." Banfield sounded patronizing but was obviously pleased. From that moment he ignored Matthew. "Who else was with you when these differences were demonstrated, Miss Canning?"

"My mother—and my brother."

"All four of you!" Banfield couldn't have looked more satisfied if he had been a cat. "So no one in the household is likely to confuse one plant with the other—is that your opinion?"

"They might—forget."

"Yes, yes, of course." Banfield relaxed, Matthew expected more questions, about the atmosphere at the house, but they didn't come. "Thank you, Miss Canning. Where can I find you? There is no one at your home just now, and as soon as you are able to see your mother, I'd like to inform you."

"You can't stay with Mrs. Dale to-night," Matthew put in.

"I'll stay with Peggy, she'll be glad to put me up," Celia said. "Take me there, will you, Matt?" She closed her eyes. "That's Miss Peggy Graham, 17 Leyden Crescent."

"Make a note of that address, Sergeant," Banfield was brisk and spuriously considerate. "Let me drive you there, Miss Canning."

"I'll drive her." Matthew was sharp.

"Very well," Banfield said. "Believe me, if I can help in any way, I will. And as soon as I have news of your father, I'll advise you. Good-bye for the present." He nodded distantly to Matthew, and turned towards the door which the sergeant had already opened for him.

When it closed, Matthew stood with a hand on Celia's shoulder. Her hand moved, crept up to his, and covered it. She looked straight ahead of her.

"There was no need—" Matthew began.

"Yes, there was," Celia said. Her voice was so low-pitched that Matthew had to strain to hear. "We've got to find out the truth, Matt. What's the use of trying to hide anything? She hates him. I've known that for years. I've often worried —she could be so venomous. If she did this—" she faltered, he felt her body grow tense. He moved, went down on one knee, and held her very tightly. "Matt, if she's tried to kill him, why should I try to help her? Why *should* I? Dad would say: 'Whatever happens, stick to the truth. It may seem to hurt but it won't hurt so much as a lie, in the long run.' He's right, you know he is. And I can imagine—" she caught her breath. "I can imagine that if Bob—if Bob did this other thing and they knew, she would be terrified in case Dad told the police. She'd do anything to save him, to save Bob. Matt, she would."

"We don't know that she did," Matthew said. His throat felt tight. "Don't let Banfield get away with too much. He's scared you. Get legal advice."

Celia said: "Matt, do what you think's best, I'll do whatever you say. Only don't ask me to lie or pretend. If—if Dad dies, I—"

She began to cry.

19

ADVICE

"There's only one thing to do," Weston said, leaning against the mantelpiece of the big, bare bedroom at the *George & Dragon*, where Matthew had decided to stay. It was half-past seven. Celia was as well cared for at the Leyden Crescent house as she could be anywhere. Matthew had taken her there, talked to plump, willing Peggy Graham, felt torn between staying with her and trying to find out what was happening. He had learned nothing more.

"Get legal advice," Weston urged. "Both Mrs. Canning and the kid need it desperately. They're still at the police station."

"What's that likely to mean?"

"Banfield may have more on them than we know, or may just be trying to break them down." Weston pulled out his pipe. "It's anyone's guess. He's fond of steam-rollering. He can get away with that in small stuff, but if you know of a lawyer who'll be tough with him, it would help."

"I think I do. Merrydew," Matthew went on. "You don't know him. He's a friend of George Canning, too."

"Try him. Like me to be there when you talk about it?"

"I'd rather you were digging for evidence. Is anything more known about Bob and—and Peter's murder?"

Weston said: "Grant, listen. Bob Canning and Cyril Rigby plotted together, and there's not much doubt that they plotted to burgle the Dales' house. Now Rigby's dead, so one witness can't talk. Putting two and two together, I'd say that Bob confessed to his mother and father, which meant there were two more witnesses of a kind—two who could give him away, anyhow. They could be deadly. If the mother were prepared to side with Bob and the father wasn't —everything I've heard about Canning suggests that he wouldn't—then there's a strong motive for mother and son to act together. They'd want it to appear accidental. Horseradish has been confused with monkshood often enough, sometimes with fatal results. Miss Canning's statement made it pretty clear that no one at the house would have confused them. I think they'll both be held on a murder charge—Rigby's murder, of course, Canning's still alive."

"Two murders to hide one," Matthew said heavily. "It's fantastic."

"Not with a little squirt like Bob Canning and a strong-minded woman who's become warped and neurotic," Weston said. "And if they knew Bob had killed Peter and there was a fight going on about whether to tell the police, you can imagine they were pretty well keyed up. You yourself know that neither Mrs. Canning nor the kid will touch horseradish sauce. No wonder Banfield thinks he's on a good thing." He paused, rubbing the bowl of his pipe. "There's only one factor which can't be worked in easily."

"What's that?"

"Waclow's fifty pounds," Weston said unexpectedly.

"Couldn't he have taken that earlier? The day he left for this holiday, for instance."

"I suppose he could. I've had another talk with his wife, saying that I thought there was a good chance that the murder charge wouldn't stick, and he'd be released on that count. She swears that he didn't take any money. It's one of these cases of blindly passionate loyalty, but she impressed me. She says that Waclow's just naturally honest." Weston smiled faintly. "I know other people like that. I've been trying to find out whether Bob Canning or this Rigby fellow knew Waclow, and whether he helped them at all. I'd say that he didn't—his broken English wouldn't make him a very good accomplice. I'd like a talk with the Pole, but Banfield will hold him right to the last minute. You see what all this means, don't you?"

Matthew said: "If Waclow didn't take the money, someone put it there."

"Right first time. Now you've got over the 'shield Miss Canning from hurt at all costs' angle, your mind's working better!" The smile robbed the words of any offence. "Then who? Not Bob Canning."

"Judging from his reputation—"

"Be logical." Weston anticipated what he was going to say. "If he'd thought of it, Bob would have framed Waclow. But the money was scattered all over the floor, wasn't it? If Bob was the thief, he'd got hold of it and was on the way out when he was interrupted. He struck, possibly killed, certainly flew into a panic. The money didn't matter to him any more, he had to get away. He isn't likely to have picked up a wad of fifty quid, stuck it in his pocket and hurried to Waclow's in-laws' home, thinking: 'This'll fix him.' Nothing that's happened suggests that Bob was in the frame of mind to be cunning, and the scattered notes make it pretty certain that he didn't do that. So we're left with this: if Waclow didn't take the fifty pounds, who hid it at his in-laws?"

"Are you getting at his wife?" Matthew asked.

"I can't see her doing that. A policeman might wonder, but I don't have to be so impartial. I'm all for the little Scots lassie. So, who?"

Matthew's thumb pressed against his forehead. He just let the thoughts pass through his mind. Weston was right about one thing, he was thinking more clearly; the news had bowled him over at first, because of the devastating blow to Celia, but now he could be dispassionate.

"So someone else might have been at Marlborough Road."

"That's it," Weston said. "I wish I knew Bob Canning's story. Banfield probably does, I fancy the little squirt would break right open under pressure. He'll swear he didn't kill, of course." The newspaperman paused. "I wish I could explain that fity pounds, too."

"Have you talked to Banfield about this?"

Weston grinned.

"Banfield thinks I'm interested in pandering to the sensational taste of newspaper readers, and that no Fleet Street journalist can be any help at all—they just get in the way. I can't say that I blame him. Will you see if this Merrydew man will act for Mrs. Canning and Bob?"

"Yes," Matthew said.

After Weston had gone, he telephoned the solicitor at his home and arranged to go there at half-past eight; Merrydew wasn't free earlier. That gave Matthew time for a hurried dinner, to go and see Celia, and then to drive to the hospital. There, they told him no more than he already knew; just that Canning was still alive.

Merrydew, a small, wizened man, in the sixties, with a widespread country practice, but little experience of criminal cases, had heard of Canning's illness but not what had followed. He promised to go to see Banfield at once; he didn't say so, but it was obvious that his chief concern was for George Canning. Unable to rest, Matthew went back *via* the hospital, and recognized Dr. Hall's Wolseley in the drive. He didn't harass the night receptionist but hung about until the old doctor came out, walking rather heavily down the steps to his car. The light from the hospital itself was poor, and Hall peered short-sightedly at Matthew.

"Yes?"

"I'm Matthew Grant—friend of Celia Canning," Matthew said; he had met the doctor two or three times. "How is Mr. Canning, please?"

"Oh," said Dr. Hall. "Yes, I recognize you. How's George Canning? I wouldn't like to say he'll pull through but he's got more chance now than he had a few hours ago."

"So he's no worse?"

"He's not even so bad. How's that girl of his? Looking after her all right?"

"I'm doing the best I can."

"It will have to be very good." Hall was gruff. "She wants to see her father, of course. Well, she mustn't. That's for two reasons. She couldn't help him and he's not nice to see at the moment. And the police are hovering about, waiting for him to come round. That wouldn't do her any good, would it?"

"Hardly."

"Can I give you a lift anywhere?" Hall asked.

"I've my own car here, thanks," Matthew said.

He drove off after the doctor, through the quiet town. Ten minutes later he was with Celia, able to give her some grounds for hope. Her eyes looked enormous in her colourless face, but she was taking all this better, far better, than Jerry Dale had taken his shock. Jerry had gone to pieces completely. Matthew felt a sense of futility and failure; the band-leader had used him as a leaning post, and the post had suddenly been taken away.

"I ought to go and see Jerry," he said to Celia. "Why don't you go to bed, darling?"

"I will, as soon as you've gone." She brushed hair back from her forehead. "Peggy's had her doctor in to see me, he's giving me a sleeping draught. I don't want to sleep, but—" she shrugged. "I don't want to do anything except pray for Dad." Her hold on his hands was very tight. "Do you *know* what's happening to Mother and Bob?"

"Merrydew will do everything he can," Matthew assured her. He could understand her distress, her divided thoughts. She ought to be distressed for her mother and brother, but couldn't find it in her. Only Canning counted.

Matthew left, remembering one good thing—the glow in her eyes when he had told her what Hall had said.

It wasn't far to the Dales' house. Last night, right up to four o'clock that afternoon for that matter, this had seemed the home of tragedy which nothing could offset. Now the disaster which had overwhelemed Celia had made Matthew forget it for hours. The light was on in a downstairs room. He did not particularly want to see old Dale; with luck, he had retired early. Mrs. Dale was better to-day, Matthew knew, and a sister had arrived to keep her company; Celia was no longer needed.

When he switched off the engine, he heard the notes of a saxophone; some mournful melody. It stopped as he approached the door. Jerry opened the door, saxophone in one hand.

"Oh, hallo," he said. He wasn't particularly enthusiastic. "I thought you'd deserted us completely." He drew aside for Matthew to enter. He knew what had kept Matthew away, yet could talk like that. Matthew followed him into the small room, half wishing he hadn't come. Jerry had been the leader of his band, Peter the man who had run the business side. As brothers, they could hardly have been more different; in a way they were rather like Celia and Bob, it was hard to believe that they were so closely related.

"Sorry," he said shortly. "I was with Celia."

"Oh, I know," Jerry said, as if he repented the sourness. He put the saxophone on a chair, where it gleamed in the light. "It's just that I—well, you know." The electric light made him look pasty, there was no colour in his cheeks and his small mouth was pale too. "I keep hearing a lot of damned silly rumours."

"Do you?"

"It was obviously Waclow, why don't the police get on with their job?" Jerry complained. He was pouring out whisky. "Usual for you?" Matthew said: "Yes, thanks." "I can't understand it. That chap Weston was here for an hour, he left about seven. He talks too much."

"Does he?" Matthew took his drink. "Thanks."

"Can't see what you like about him," Jerry muttered. "Cheers. He says he thinks there's someone else they suspect, now. One of those kids." Jerry moved his glass round, watching the whisky and soda move up and down the side of the glass. "It's crazy—it *must* have been Waclow."

"The main thing is to get the right man, surely."

"They've got him, I tell you! I was pretty sure it was that Polish swine all the time. I never liked him. Father made a mistake employing him, you can't trust these chaps. If he didn't do it, how did he get hold of that money? Tell me that."

"That's what's puzzling Weston."

"So he's been at you about that, has he?" Jerry growled. He drained his glass. "Shall I be glad when all this is over! Dragging it on like this is killing the old folk—and it isn't helping Peter!" He poured himself out another drink and forced a grin. "Not much company, am I? I feel so damned awful about the whole business. I just can't rest." He sipped. "Er—how's Celia's father?"

"There's some hope."

"Oh, that's fine," Jerry forced enthusiasm. "That's wonderful. I'm a selfish brute, can't think of anything but my own troubles. What I'm going to do without Peter I can't imagine. He was—oh, what's the use of talking?"

He went on talking, all the same, was pathetically anxious for Matthew not to go. It was after midnight before Matthew finally left, with a mixed feeling of guilt at having booked the room at the *George & Dragon* and satisfaction at not having to sit long into the small hours while Jerry went on being sorry for himself.

There wasn't much genuine grief in Jerry; he was shocked and sorry for himself. What did people really think about? What was Celia thinking, for instance—and what had Canning thought when he realized that he had been poisoned? Had his wife—

The saxophone started afresh.

Matthew stabbed at the self-starter, forced the thoughts away and drove too quickly out of the grounds. He slowed down soon, and drove past the house where Celia was staying. No lights were on anywhere; that was probably a good sign.

He parked the car in the yard of the *George & Dragon*, went in, and saw Weston getting up from one of the big armchairs which the hotel boasted. Weston didn't look tired or excited, but gave the impression that he had good news.

"What's on?" Matthew asked abruptly.

"Canning's out of danger," Weston told him. "We should know in the morning whether he can help the police."

20

RECOVERY

CANNING knew that he was alive; and he felt no pain. There was only a great listlessness and numbness, as if all sensation had been drawn out of his body. His mind was hazy and confused. Although vague, half-formed thoughts entered it, they vanished without his making any attempt to hold them. His chief awareness was of release from pain. Nothing hurt him any more. He did not feel fear; did not think of the possibility of dying.

He dozed off, half an hour or so after he had first come round, vaguely aware that someone was with him but with no clear idea who it was.

When he came round next, his mind cleared much more quickly and his thoughts were more sharply defined. His stomach ached; so did his throat; and there was an unfamiliar taste in his mouth. He felt limp, and whenever he moved his arms it was with an effort which he quickly decided was not worth making.

He was alone in a small ward, but was not left alone for long. A nurse came in. He focused his gaze on her, but could not be sure whether she was young or old, only that she was in white. Her voice sounded a long way off.

"How are you feeling, Mr. Canning?"

He looked at her, puzzled. Then he realized that he had to answer a civil question. He started to speak, and the first effort brought pain to his throat and reminded him of what had happened at the house. His muscles were slack, but he felt the urge of fear. The nurse smiled and went out; soon she was back with a man who came quickly to Canning's side, took his right hand and pressed his wrist with a forefinger, smiled down and said:

"You're going to be all right. You've nothing to worry about now."

So he had nothing to worry about; just the agony of knowing that he had been poisoned, that Bob or Belle had tried to kill him. From that moment on he remembered everything, as he would have done had he woken out of a deep sleep. All the emotions, the fears and hopes, were back; except that hope was much, much weaker.

He wanted desperately to know what had happened but he did not want to ask the doctor.

They gave him something to drink, and left him, but not for long.

Soon, he drifted into sleep again.

When he came round, he knew that he had made another stride forward; he was still limp, but did not feel the same unconquerable inertia. His mind was fully alert. He recalled the first stabs of pain, the shock of realizing that he had been poisoned. It became extremely important for him to know what had happened to Belle. He waited tensely for a nurse or the doctor to come, but this time they left him alone for a long time. He was becoming angry with impatience when the door opened. A nurse came in.

"Hallo, Mr. Canning, how—"

"I want to see my wife." His voice was weak but the words were audible.

"We'll arrange that as soon as we can," the nurse said. He watched her face for any tell-tale signs, but she was quite calm. "Your daughter is coming to see you this morning."

"Celia?" Celia, of course! She would tell him what had happened.

He convinced himself that he was quite cool about it all. Dispassionate. Either Belle or Bob had poisoned him. The police must know that, and would have taken some action by now. He realized that the police would soon question him, and until he knew what action they had taken, he would not answer their questions. If Celia came before the police he would have a chance to think out his answers.

The police came first.

There was Banfield himself and a wooden-looking man in blue who sat some distance from the bed with a notebook on his knees. Banfield was his ruddy, if subdued, self. He shook hands gently, said how delighted he was that Canning had recovered; that all his friends were greatly relieved, too. He, Banfield, wished that he hadn't to ask questions but he was sure that Canning would tell him what he could. There was no need to worry, now. Did he remember—

"Where is my wife?" Canning asked, clearly.

"Listen, George, it's important that you should answer just a few questions before you start worrying about anything else. Do you remember what happened just before you were taken ill?"

Canning looked at him stubbornly, but didn't speak.

"We know that the poison was in the sauce, monkshood had been used as well as horseradish. It was a hell of a thing to happen, George, although it's not the first time. I'm not sure I shall be so fond of horseradish in the future!" Banfield showed his big teeth in a persuasive smile. "Who mixed the sauce, do you know?"

"I want to see my wife," Canning said.

"Yes, George, as soon as—"

"*And* my daughter."

"I think Celia's on the way here," Banfield said. "If she isn't, she soon will be. Do you remember who mixed the sauce yesterday?"

Yes, Canning remembered, but did not have to answer. Belle had asked him to make sure that Bob had mixed it. Bob. That did not have any particular effect on him. He felt very clear-headed, and knew that it might have been either Bob or Belle. A husband could not be compelled to give evidence against his wife, could he?

"I've nothing to say, Ted."

"Listen, George—"

"Where is my wife? Why isn't she here? You said you'd thought Celia was on the way. But why isn't Belle here? She's all right, isn't she?"

"She's perfectly well. George, try to help. I've my job to do, you know and we have to find out how that mistake occurred. Who mixed the sauce?"

"Why don't you stop worrying me?" Canning asked, very slowly and deliberately. "I don't know who mixed it."

He doubted whether Banfield would have given up then, but a doctor came in. Both the policemen went out, and Canning felt a futile kind of satisfaction at having fooled Banfield. Then his thoughts settled into sombre mould. It was as if he had had some prevision, and knew the whole truth. If Belle were being held, why hadn't Banfield admitted it? Or Bob, for that matter.

A nurse brought him a drink and some milk food. He had only just finished it when she came back again; this time Celia was behind her.

Canning lay back on his pillows, looking at his daughter, all the strength gone from him. The attack of weakness made his eyes smart and his lips tremble. Celia moved slowly at first; next moment she was kneeling by the bed. His arm went round her, not tightly, because he had so little strength. Her strong young body was heavy against his, and suddenly she seemed to realize that, and drew away.

She still held his hands. Her eyes were filmed with tears and her cheeks were wet. She sniffed.

"It's all right, it's all right," Canning said huskily. "Don't fret, my darling. Everything will be all right."

"Of—of course it will." Her voice was unsteady and the tears welled up again. "I'm so silly. If I go on like this they won't let me come again."

"Let them try to stop you," Canning said. There was no strength in his voice, but plenty in his mind. They fell silent for a while and then the old question stirred, and he had to speak of it. "Where's your mother, Celia? And Bob?"

"Oh—Dad." She choked.

"Tell me," Canning urged her. "I can guess that it isn't good. Ted Banfield has as much tact as an ox. What's happened to them, Celia?"

"They—" she caught her breath, then words rushed out. "The police think they did it. It was in the horseradish sauce."

"Monkshood. Yes. Remember I gave you a demonstration about that in the autumn." Canning smiled faintly, but his lips felt very stiff. "Are they under arrest?"

"Yes," she whispered. "They were arrested this morning."

"Have you seen either of them?"

"The police won't let me." Celia went on very quickly. "I don't know that I want to, I shouldn't know what to say. If they did—"

"I can guess how you feel," said Canning gently. He felt very tired, and fell silent again. Then: "Celia, I had a feeling that your mother had changed. That's why I said nothing about Bob before." He talked as if she knew everything about the ordeal at the house. "I wanted to tell the police that he'd been to the Dales' house, but she wouldn't let me. She changed her mind, though. Or—I thought she had." He was looking into Celia's eyes, and something there told him that this was news to her. "Of course, you didn't know!"

"I—was afraid that it was—was something like that."

"Has Bob been charged with that—that band-player's murder too?"

"I don't think so, Dad. I'd know if he had been, I think. There's Mr. Merrydew, who's acting for them—for us. And Mr. Weston, he came to see you, didn't he? He's a great help. Dad, are you sure Bob killed Peter?"

"Nearly sure. I'm sure he thinks he did, anyhow," Canning said, "and perhaps that means that he meant to. I can't rely on anything he says, but that's no change. Celia, listen—listen, my darling." She held her breath as she looked at him. "Bob mixed that sauce. Your mother asked me to make sure that he'd done it. Would she have asked, if she'd known what was in it? Bob—yes, I'm resigned to Bob being ready to murder me, but Belle—" He broke off. "Tell Merrydew that." His voice strengthened. "Have the police been worrying you?"

"Not really. Banfield's been—very considerate."

"So I should think."

Then silence fell. When Canning stirred, it was to press her hand, and to say:

"Celia, we've got to be sure about your mother. After what we'd agreed, I can't believe that she—that she knew about it. Help her, my darling. If I were able to, I'd help, I'd do anything—"

Celia began to cry again, silently. Then the door opened and the doctor appeared. The nurse followed. Canning felt as if their coming had suddenly sapped his strength, and his hand fell limp. He felt Celia kiss his forehead, but when he opened his eyes, she had gone. There was the smiling doctor, a youngish man, and the nurse with some medicine which wasn't too bad to taste.

"No more visitors to-day," the doctor announced. "But if it helps at all, Mr. Canning, I can tell you that you've many friends in Minchester and they all want to help. A lot are trying to. Try to take a nap, now, you'll feel much better next time you wake up."

Would he?

Oddly, Canning felt that it was good that he could not really summon all his energies even to worry about Belle. That was a nagging uncertainty, no more. One of them had tried to kill him, but what reason could Belle have? Bob would have been glad to see him dead; his 'friend' dead, too. Canning realized that he hadn't asked how the unspeakable Cyril was.

It occurred to him that Cyril might have died, and that would mean there was a charge of murder against Belle, if it were taken so far. Even that did not stir him out of a creeping drowsiness. They'd drugged him, of course.

What—could—he—do—to—help—Belle?

After that, his thoughts were hazy and he felt little emotion.

It would be a dreadful thing if Belle were blamed for poisoning him when Bob had done it. The way to help Belle was to find out the truth. Who would do that? What did she feel like, now that he wasn't at hand?

He went to sleep.

The doctor had been right; when he woke up, he felt much better—refreshed as well as more in control of his limbs and thoughts. A dim electric light was on; so it was night time. He lay unmoving for a while, then stirred and rang for a nurse. One came in quickly.

It was five o'clock, she told him, dawn would soon break. Was there anything he wanted?

"I'm feeling hungry," Canning said, as if that surprised him.

She smiled. "I'll soon put that right!" She went off, and came back with some pappy milk broth, and propped him up to eat it.

Soon afterwards, he heard the birds stirring; and remembered their chorus on the morning that Bob had come home to begin all this. He pictured the way Belle had behaved; and went over her changes of mood and behaviour all the time. He could not bring himself to believe that she had deceived him. Face it, face it—she wasn't a fool, if she had wanted to kill him, she wouldn't have done it that way, would she? It had been idiocy. Bob hadn't any sense, only an almost animal cunning. He would think of something, remember the lecture on monkshood and, as he had at the Dales' house, do just whatever came into his head. Belle would see every move in advance. But what would she do now? Above everything else she loved Bob, she had tried desperately to save him; and she might be prepared to sacrifice herself for him.

"No!" exclaimed Canning, aloud.

It was from that moment that he really began to exert himself, for his wife's sake.

21

HOME AGAIN

CANNING looked out of the window of the car, mildly surprised by the changes in the countryside in the three weeks that he had been away. Trees and hedges were in full leaf, fields which had looked bare and barren were covered with a carpet of green shoots. The gardens outside the cottages in the villages were different, too; only a few tulips were left, and here and there straggly wallflowers; the daffodils were gone. Smaller flowers, promise of summer, gave colour to the morning.

It was a warm day; May as hot as May could be, with a few wispy white clouds drifting across the sky. The ground looked hard; there had been little rain while Canning had been in hospital.

Randall sat with him in the back of the large Rolls Royce, humbled to a taxi rank; they had said little. Turning the corner by the garage and the lamp, Canning saw that many of the pit-holes in the private road had been filled in, a steam-roller had been at work. The gardens on either side were ablaze with colour. It was eleven o'clock, and many neighbours were gardening. Several stopped to look, but did not wave.

The old Rolls Royce pulled up at the gates of *Hillview*.

"Open the gates, and drive right up," Randall ordered the driver.

"No," Canning said vigorously. "I'll walk. I want to walk. I'm not decrepit yet."

Randall shrugged, and the driver helped Canning out. There was little need. He had been well enough to come home a week ago, but had taken Dr. Hall's advice to stay and regain his strength. He felt fit, and had walked round the hospital grounds; but for the burning anxiety of mind because of the failure of his fight for Belle, he would have been content. As it was, there was a kind of happiness in him. The garden had been well tended; on most days, two or three friends from Minchester had driven out for a couple of hours, doing quite as much as he and Belle could have. The lawn was trim and cleanly edged. Antirrhinums and asters, not yet in flower, filled the beds, where colour came from the dusting blue of forget-me-nots and the powdery pink London Pride. Violets, too, were blooming, and some of the flowering bushes still held their blossom.

The door opened.

Celia came running down the drive, and Matthew stood in the porch, leaving her to go alone. Her cheeks were bright and her eyes eager. Canning watched her, satisfaction welling up. In spite of everything she looked happy; and in one way at least, she was. The sun flashed on the diamond ring on her engagement finger and the slender platinum ring beside it.

Celia was married; and deep down, Canning was glad.

"Oh, Dad, it's good to see you!" She hugged him, and kissed him full on the lips. "You look *fine*." She held his arms and stood back, to study him. "You've been out in the sun, you've quite a colour!"

"Anyone would think that you hadn't seen me every day for the past three weeks," growled Canning. "You don't look ailing yourself." He glanced towards Matthew, and waved. Matthew approached. "How's my new son-in-law?"

"Wonderful!"

"I'd better get a dispassionate opinion." Canning shook hands with Matthew. "Matt, it was good of you to be here this morning."

"Any excuse for a day off," Matthew said lightly. "Good morning, Mr. Randall."

"'Morning, you youngsters. George, you'll have to forgive me, I've a busy day at the office," Randall said. "We can't all play ducks and drakes with our business like these young people." He winked at Matthew, squeezed Celia's hand. "Look after him. No, George, I really must go."

He turned and hurried away, and Canning watched him go. The Rolls Royce had already been turned round, and they were soon on their way.

"Coffee's on," Celia said, when they turned back towards the house. "Would you like to have it out here in the garden, Dad?"

"Certainly not," Canning was still gruff. "You two go and amuse yourselves for ten minutes, will you?"

They went off, towards the back of the house. The front door was wide open. Canning walked slowly towards it. It was difficult to believe that Belle would not appear, if only for a moment—to glare at him in some moods and to wave in others. In spite of his battle for her, it was difficult not to see her glaring, with that icy expression in her eyes, more clearly than it was to see her smile. In his heart he could not make up his mind about Belle; to feel that she and Bob had poisoned him between them, or to believe that she was saying nothing in her own defence, for Bob's sake.

He went in. Everything was exactly as he remembered it. Why not? Had he been away for years? He smiled, tensely. The doors were open and the curtains in the drawing-room were pulled, to keep out the sun and save the furniture and carpet from fading. He went in and looked round, then began a tour of the house, without quite knowing what urged him to do that. In a way, it was as if he were looking for Belle.

Celia's room was different. Matthew's bed had been brought across from the other room, and was pushed close to hers. Canning's smile softened.

They had been married a week.

Matthew had visited him to ask whether he would object, but before then, Celia had told him the simple truth.

"He just wants to make me—and you—realize that he doesn't care about other things."

"It's only bringing things forward a few months, and both of us would like to be together more," Matthew had said. "It's difficult for Celia just now."

"Difficult for Celia" was one way of putting it. Canning

had been able to imagine what she had felt like. Everyone who saw her knew that her mother and brother were in the County Gaol, awaiting trial on a charge of murdering Cyril Rigby and attempting to murder Canning. Matthew had been fiercely anxious to show Minchester and the world, for that matter, that he hadn't changed towards Celia. Knowing that, it had been easy for Canning to say yes. They snatched at life, having felt its waywardness. They lived for the day and troubled not about to-morrow for they had faith together.

He wondered what Belle thought of the marriage.

If Belle came home—yes, the doubt was there and he faced it—then the youngsters would live in Minchester.

If Belle did not come home. . . .

He went into his study, and sat down heavily. The manuscripts on which he had been working when Weston had called were in neat piles. The furniture had been polished, but nothing had been moved out of place. There was a large pile of unopened letters; another of letters which had been acknowledged by Matthew or by Celia.

Now that he was sitting down, he felt too tired to get up; suddenly weary and sick at heart. He heard the others moving about below. God give them happiness, grant that Celia would never change as—

He tried to shut the thought out, but couldn't. There had been nothing to suggest that Belle could ever change as she had. Why *had* she changed? How much of it was due to Bob's coming?

He tried to imagine them both in prison, what they must be feeling; and began to think again over what had passed.

They had been charged with the murder of Cyril Rigby at a special Magistrates' Court, remanded for eight days, brought up again and committed for trial at the County Assizes; that was due in two week's time.

Merrydew had told Canning much more. He was astonished at how much the police had discovered, and at the distressing evidence of Belle's moods, of the atmosphere in this house. Apparently Banfield would produce surprising witnesses—all with the purpose of showing that Belle hated her husband.

The story of Peter Dale's murder and Bob's part in it had come out at the inquest, not always referred to directly.

Merrydew had pointed out something which Canning might not have discovered so easily for himself: there was never any implicit statement that Bob had killed Peter Dale, and he had not been charged with that. Bob had made a long statement to the police, most of it true, describing what had happened at *Hillview*. The evidence of Belle's hatred for her husband had been built up on that statement.

Belle had not said a word in court, except to plead 'not guilty' on Merrydew's urgent request. Canning understood that there had been a time when she had refused even to do that. Bob had broken down in dock; it must have been a shocking exhibition. Most of the newspapers had played it up strongly. ACCUSED YOUTH SOBS IN DOCK. HYSTERICAL BOY SCREAMS NOT GUILTY. In a wild statement he had sworn that he knew nothing about the monkshood, that his mother had told him to scrape the horseradish and make the sauce, told him how to do it, and where to get the plant from the vegetable bin in the kitchen. Not by word or gesture had he done anything which would help his mother.

What did Belle think about that? What a bitter reward, for her years of doting!

Another thing had happened, not surprising in itself, although there was a puzzling consequence. Waclow had been freed from the charge of murdering Peter Dale but held on a charge of robbery from his employer. He was also awaiting trial, at the Assizes. The puzzle was that Bob hadn't been charged with Peter's murder; that no one had. Merrydew had said that Banfield was more certain of a conviction on the other charge, and was leaving the first in abeyance. No one who read the newspapers could have much doubt that Bob had killed Peter Dale.

Now they could only wait.

Canning had not seen Belle, although Merrydew had assured him that there would be no difficulty, once he felt that he could bring himself to. No difficulty, that was, from the legal point of view; whether Belle would see him was a different matter. She had refused to see anyone—Celia had not been able to see her, although she had tried several times.

"How is she?" Canning had asked Merrydew, feeling almost desperate.

"I think she's very well in health, George. She's quite composed. She isn't willing to talk, won't do anything to help herself. She won't even talk to me." And then he had added something which he probably regretted afterwards, although Canning was glad that it had been said: "It's almost as if she wants to die. If she keeps it up, it will probably be taken as a confession of guilt."

Even in hospital, surrounded by nurses and watched carefully, it was surprising how news of many things had reached Canning. They had tried to keep the newspapers from him, but other patients hadn't been so futile. Patients, even some nurses, had talked. The police had called several times; Banfield had become more and more embarrassed and yet still dogged; Canning had said nothing more than he had at the first interview. Celia had been questioned, he knew, and she had told Canning what she had said about the monkshood demonstration; and why.

"Of course you are right, don't think twice about it," he had said. Yet it had hurt, because undoubtedly she had talked out of the bitterness which she had felt for her mother. She could not really pretend to feel grief for Belle, although after the shock, she had tried hard enough.

She called up from the foot of the stairs.

"Are you coming down, or shall I bring coffee up?"

"Will you bring it, dear?"

"Coming!"

She came with Matthew, carrying three cups of creamy-looking coffee. There were only two chairs; Matthew sat on a corner of the desk. The same thought was in all their minds, of course; they would soon have to talk about 'it' again; pretending that things were normal wouldn't last for long.

"What happened to that newspaperman, Weston?" Canning asked. "I haven't heard much about him for the past week or so."

"He was called back to London," Matthew said. "He telephones me every other evening, he's still interested." Matthew didn't say so, but the kindliest handling of the inquest and the Magistrates' Court hearing had been by Weston in the *Clarion*. "He always doubted whether Waclow was guilty. In fact I'm not sure that Banfield would have got on to Bob about Peter's murder if it hadn't been for Weston. I don't know, though, they found out about the bicycle."

"It had Bob's prints on it, of course," Canning said. "Well, I suppose we've got to live with it for a bit longer. I wish your mother would say something, I'd feel better if I thought she—" he broke off.

Celia said quietly: "You still love her very much, don't you?" She spoke quietly, as if there were something which she could not understand.

"Yes," Canning said slowly. "Yes. I suppose I do."

It wasn't quite so simple as that. He had loved her, and had felt hope, exciting, exhilarating hope, that she would come back to him as she had once been. Hope died hard.

"I'll just have to see her, somehow. I've a feeling that if I could, she might talk. Merrydew is coming out this evening, we'll discuss it then. That means that you two can have an evening off, if you feel like it!"

"We don't feel like it," Matthew said, giving his slow smile. "You can't shake us off as easily as that."

Canning forced a grin.

Then there came a ring at the front-door bell, sharp and piercing. It jolted Canning back to the moment of fear when the bell had rung before. He started violently. Matthew stood up from the desk, and said: "I'll go." Canning watched him go out and listened as he went quietly down the stairs; strained his ears to catch his words after he had opened the door. It wasn't much strain, for Matthew exclaimed:

"Good lord, what's brought you back?" He called upstairs. "It's Mr. Randall."

"Jim?" Canning moved. "He's hardly had time to get to Minchester and back. Come up, Jim. Can you find another cup of coffee, Celia?"

"Yes, of course," She jumped up.

Randall and Matthew came in. Celia didn't go, after all, for Randall's expression stopped her. He looked bewildered, obviously had news of importance, and was as obviously at a loss for words.

"What's brought you, Jim?"

"I just had to come and see you," Randall said, and swallowed hard. "Didn't want to telephone or let someone else bring the news."

He hesitated, and Canning thought:

"Something's happened to Belle." His thoughts flashed to suicide.

"What—"

"Jerry Dale has been charged with his brother's murder," Randall said.

22

ONE MURDERER

SILENCE fell upon the room.

All three of the others watched Canning, Celia holding her breath, as if she were terrified of the effect of this. Randall, looking too hot in a tweed suit, wiped his neck slowly, and then dabbed his forehead. Matthew stood by the open door, very still. Canning turned slowly away from Randall, and looked at Celia. Did she know what this meant?

Could even he *realize* it?

For a few moments he could not think clearly; the significance had come with a flash of revelation, and then his mind seemed to stop working. Gradually, it began to work again, and a wave of emotion followed. Jerry Dale had been charged with his brother's murder. Banfield dared not make a mistake about that, any mistake was unthinkable so—Jerry had killed his brother. *Bob hadn't.* None of this had been necessary, there had been no real danger for the boy.

Think.

His son was a murderer.

There had been no need to poison him and Cyril, no need to try to make sure of their silence.

Hurt came, slowly at first, and spread as if it were a physical thing, pressing against Canning's nerves and his muscles in a great ache which made his body sag. This dreadful irony, this awful, hideous joke.

Randall broke the silence, awkwardly.

"Jerry has confessed."

No one else spoke. Randall's round, fresh face had lost all its brightness and confidence, he looked almost as stricken as Canning. Celia moved to Matthew's side, and their hands clasped.

Randall went on: "I didn't get back to town. Had to telephone the office, and they told me. Jerry was arrested early this morning. Banfield has issued a statement to the Press but he told Merrydew more, and Merrydew was at my office. I don't know all about it, but apparently Jerry had been squandering the band's money, had got himself heavily into debt." Randall paused, and Canning thought, as far as it was possible for him to think: "Another son." He hardly saw Randall or any of the others, only the pasty face of the band-leader, his small lips and smarmed hair. "Some time before, he'd stolen his mother's jewels, pledged them and hoped to get them back. There's more to it, of course, but that's the general position. Peter was taken ill with that attack of malaria and Jerry sent him home. Even before that, Jerry had planted money in Waclow's suit-case—we know about that now. He was going to stage a burglary and have Waclow blamed for everything—including the jewel theft.

"He got to the house, after the dance that night, and found Peter unconscious on the floor, with money about everywhere. Peter came round. Somehow he had found out what Jerry had done with the jewels, and accused him of staging the robbery to cover up the other crimes. Jerry killed him. He used Waclow's knife, he'd stolen that to prise open locks and to strengthen the evidence against Waclow. He took away another knife—Peter's."

Randall stopped; but couldn't keep quiet for long.

"Dreadful story, dreadful." He fingered his chin. "I couldn't let that—that news reach you in a roundabout way, George, could I?" It was a plea, that he should not be blamed; saying that he hated the need for it. "So—Bob *didn't* kill Peter."

Canning stood up, very slowly, went past Celia and Matthew to the window and looked out over the garden which he and Belle had tended for so many years. He saw the distant trees, where they hid the quarry. The roofs of the houses were almost hidden by the leaves now. He stood quite still.

"Is there anything I can *do*?" Randall burst out.

"No, Mr. Randall, no." Celia spoke. "You've been very good. Father will understand if—"

"Yes, I must go. No doubt about it, Celia, understand that. Jerry's confessed." He looked at Matthew as if for sympathy. "I must go." He moved towards the door, and Matthew let Celia's hand go and followed him.

Canning knew that they had gone out of the room, although he hardly heard a sound. He had heard little of Randall's story, only the essential facts had made any impression on his whirling mind. Bob had not killed Peter Dale, there had been no need for his terror, no need for that awful struggle with Belle, no need—no need to poison him. Or Cyril Rigby. Needless fear of the gallows had driven Bob or Belle to the final act. *Bob or Belle?* The question screamed at him. Bob denied it wildly, hysterically; let his mother hang, he didn't care; he would have denied it whether he had mixed that sauce or not. He would see his mother, see anyone die so as to save himself.

Bob or Belle?

Canning felt Celia brush againt him as she reached his side. He didn't turn to look at her, but she changed the direction of his thoughts, gave him the first moment of relief. What could she be thinking? The same things, of course; she would be equally appalled by the horror of it.

He must see Belle; someone must make her agree to see him. It was no use seeing Bob, he would never be able to judge from his son whether it was the truth or not; he would assume that it was a lie. But he was sure that he could tell whether Belle was lying. He remembered the way she had turned on him, and threatened to kill him; then the gradual thawing of her manner, the softening; and that had been spoiled by her manner when she had been left alone with Bob, especially the morning that Cyril Rigby had come. First fear; then soon afterwards, Cyril smug and Bob less frightened than usual, almost gloating.

If Bob had known what was in the horseradish sauce, could he have been so calm?

Bob or Belle?

There were voices downstairs, and they broke the quiet of the room. They drew nearer. Canning thought, vaguely, that Randall hadn't gone, then realized that the voice besides Matthew's wasn't Randall's. It was a brisker voice, and deeper; the voice of a man who didn't waste words. Merrydew. Canning turned from the window with an effort. Merrydew, a dried-up looking man with big eyes and long lashes, an old man with a child's eyes, came in as if he were determined not to let anyone keep him out. He was very thin, with sunken cheeks, a leathery, monkeyish face. He wore a black coat, a wing collar, grey cravat and striped trousers. He came across at once.

"Good morning, Celia. Hallo, George. Randall's been here, I understand. I thought I passed him on the road."

"Yes, Lionel."

"I think this might be the opportunity to make your wife

talk," Merrydew said, "and I think she's more likely to talk to you than anyone else. Banfield is anxious to let you try. She doesn't know about this, yet." He paused. "Will you try to help?"

"Don't be a fool, Lionel. Of course I will." Canning's voice found a sudden strength.

"Good. Now I can't be certain but my own personal opinion of your wife's state of mind is that she is perfectly well, but determined not to make any contribution to the inquiry or her defence. My private opinion, for what it's worth, is that she is shielding her son. When she knows about this, she will realize that he is in no danger from hanging for Dale's murder and therefore the only risk is for Cyril Rigby's. If she is determined to sacrifice herself for Bob, this will only make her more determined. She'll know that she can succeed. So you have to talk to her before she finds out. And it's no use saying that she can't find out in prison, rumours get about there as well as anywhere else."

Canning said: "I suppose so." If Merrydew thought that he was contributing anything to the problem, he was wrong; of course this was exactly what Belle needed, if she were keeping quiet to save Bob—who doubtless believed he had killed Jerry Dale. Believing that, he would want to silence his father and Rigby. Once Belle knew about Jerry's arrest, nothing in the world was likely to make her implicate Bob.

"What do you suggest we do?" Canning asked.

"I want you to come into Minchester with me, at once. Come to see Belle with me. She won't know that you're coming. The surprise might shock her out of her silence. I've Banfield's promise that he'll leave the two of you together. It's entirely a matter for you, George—whether you can compel her to say what really happened. If she refuses to talk to you—" he shrugged. "I don't think we'll get her off. The evidence is damning. I don't know everything that the police have found, but from what I know I think they could convince any jury that she and Bob did this together. The jury might possibly think that she did it without Bob's knowledge. Will you come?"

"Yes," said Canning.

Celia said: "I don't care what either of you say, you're not leaving here until you've had something to eat. I'm not sure you can stand the strain, Dad, it—"

"Don't worry, Celia."

"I'll go down and get a snack," Celia said abruptly. "Matt, come and help me, will you?"

They left Canning and Merrydew, but the solicitor had nothing new to say. Canning found his thoughts going round and round the same hopeless circle. Bob or Belle? The bitterness of the new discovery had eased; what mattered was finding out the truth. If Belle would talk to him, at least he would know exactly what had happened; he had to be able to judge the truth, and had to make her talk in her own defence. If she were innocent, of course. And if she were, then she must know that Bob was prepared to let her die for a murder that he had committed. Would her love be strong enough for that?

There was no doubt; could she keep silent and go to the gallows, knowing that Bob had committed the crime and that he would live to commit more? If it had concerned anyone else, Canning would have said that the idea was fantastic, mother-love could not go that far. But with Belle and all her doting, all her blindness towards Bob—yes, it was possible.

Canning hardly knew what he was eating.

Merrydew's car was large enough for all four of them, but Matthew and Celia followed in the M.G. Merrydew was a fast driver and took risks which Canning hardly noticed. It was desperately urgent to get to Belle, and he felt that minutes might make a difference.

Merrydew had telephoned Banfield, to warn him.

They reached the High Street, went straight through it and out towards the hospital, then turned into a narrow street and reached the County Gaol, a red brick building behind high red brick walls with barbed wire on top of them. The huge gates were closed, but promptly opened for them to go through. A warder on gate duty saluted them. They parked the cars in the yard, and then were taken through huge steel barred gates, which were locked behind them, towards the offices.

Canning hadn't been here before, but he knew the elderly prison Governor, who was in his large office, with Banfield. Banfield jumped up from his chair, big face eager; he searched Canning's eyes, as if looking for signs of repugnance; blame.

"Hallo, Ted," Canning said.

"George, I can't say how sorry I am. I couldn't act before, I just couldn't get the evidence. You must be—"

The Governor broke in: "Sit down, George."

"Yes, of course," boomed Banfield. "You must be feeling pretty weak. George, I just couldn't get the evidence before." He was talking for the sake of talking, rather like Randall on occasions. "I thought it was the gardener at first but I just couldn't fit in the money it looked as if he'd stolen. Couldn't see your—your son planting it on him, so I had to look somewhere else. Mrs. Dale discovered the loss of her jewels, and it was obvious that they'd been stolen by one of the family—never mind how, we found that out. Under pressure, Jerry confessed."

Canning didn't speak.

"How soon can George see his wife?" Merrydew asked.

"Whenever you like," the Governor said.

23

TOGETHER

CANNING knew that the police would be listening to him and Belle, although no one had said so. He knew that Banfield was doubtful about her part in the poisoning; that Banfield, with all his faults, was desperately anxious not to make a mistake. Canning was not even able to think that, in spite of appearances, Banfield had not taken anything for granted; hadn't he kept at the case of Peter Dale's murder until he had worried out the truth?

So the police would be listening, and everything said by him and Belle would be taken down. Canning didn't know whether it could be used in evidence; it could certainly be used to guide the police. So it was vital that whatever Belle said should be the truth.

Above all, Canning had to be sure that it was true; to know whether Bob or Belle had tried to kill him.

Matthew and Celia were left behind. The Governor, Banfield and Merrydew walked with Canning, like guards; and a warder went ahead, with keys. The two officials stopped at a small room, and the Governor said: "We'll leave you here."

Merrydew kept very close to Canning's side as they went after the warder to another door, outside which was a second warder and a wardress—a big, red-faced woman, who stood at ease.

"She's in here," Merrydew whispered. "I'll go in first. Give me just a few seconds. Then I'll leave you together."

Canning nodded.

The wardress opened the door, and went ahead of Merrydew. He looked tiny beside her, a monkey of a man. Then she drew back into the stone-walled passage. Canning felt his heart thumping, felt his head reeling. He fought back the physical weakness, but it seemed an age before he was able to put one foot before the other and follow Merrydew.

Belle was sitting against the wall, looking at Merrydew; a Belle with no expression on her face, with her silky fair hair almost straight and tied back from her forehead, wearing one of her cotton dresses. Her hands were in her lap, she looked resigned to whatever was going to happen; in that first glimpse he was reminded vividly of Waclow.

Then she saw him.

All her repose went.

Her hands bunched in her lap. Her eyes lost the calmness, but it was impossible to judge what put the fire into them. She didn't get up. Her lips parted, and Canning could hear her breathing through them. He saw only Belle, did not know when Merrydew went out, did not hear the door close, and did not notice the small hatch on the right-hand wall, open a little at the bottom.

Words would not come. They watched each other, and the blaze faded in her eyes. Yet she was still tense, watchful, wary.

Canning prayed for the right words; for the key that would unlock her self-imposed silence. He searched her face for understanding but gained none; and still the words would not come. She was no more able to speak than he. They seemed to stay like that for an age, and the right words were not in him.

Then they came to his mind and his lips at the same time, and brought swift release from tension.

"I had to see you, Belle," he said. "I love you so much."

She sagged forward, her eyes closing, and Canning thought that she was going to faint. He moved to her quickly, went down on his knees and tried to take her hands, but they were clenched so tightly together. He covered them with his, without speaking. He felt her body trembling.

"Belle, oh, Belle."

All he could see was her fair hair, the waves at the back of her head, the skin at the nape of her neck. He pressed his lips against her hair and his hands clasped hers so tightly that it must have hurt.

"Belle, Belle."

She moved her head, very slowly. He had time to raise his. There were tears at her eyes, but they hadn't fallen. Her skin was as free from blemish as he had ever known it. And he loved her. Whatever she had done, he loved her.

"You shouldn't have come," she said in a hoarse voice, "I told them to keep you away."

"I wouldn't stay away, I made them bring me here. What do you think I'm made of, Belle? Do you think I could be in peace for a moment, without seeing you, without telling you—what I feel?" He almost shouted at her. "Do you think I would have lived with you for so long if I hadn't—"

"George, stop!"

"Why should I stop?" Suddenly he was furious; anger was the one emotion he had not expected, but then he had come without knowing what he would say or feel; had been numbed. Now rage possessed him. He had never been angry with her before, he had never shouted or lost his temper. It was as if the bottled-up rage of years came spilling out. "Isn't this a time for the truth? Sometimes I thought I hated you, wanted to be anywhere out of your sight, but I couldn't go. I *couldn't* go. Now what are you doing?" He was still on his knees but leaning back, and the words poured out. "Tell me, what are you doing? First you put me in hell. Then you made me think you were letting me out again, for the first time in years I really hoped. Now you'd damn me for the rest of my life, let me suffer the agony of your trial, of knowing you are going to be hanged. Do you think I'll let you? What do you think I am, a witless, hopeless fool? What are you going to gain from dying for a crime you didn't commit? In God's name can't you *try* to save yourself?"

He was trembling; she was shaking.

The words dried up, and some of the feeling seemed to go with them. He stood up, slowly, and moved away from her. She just sat there, looking up into his face. Now he would know what had really happened. It did not occur to him, then, that whatever she said, it would not save her; something much more was needed. But first he must know the truth.

Gradually, it came to him.

There was no guilt in her.

He felt as if he had been lifted up, as if his spirit were freed. She had not said a word but he was sure that she had not poisoned him. There was not elation but exaltation; he *knew*. This was the Belle he had dreamed of, the Belle who was truly the mother of Celia. There was no bitterness in her, either.

"Belle, what happened?" he asked huskily.

"All my life," she began, and paused. "All the life I can remember, I have tried to help him. Do you expect me to stop, now?"

But that wasn't what she meant; that was just an answer to deceive him. He felt sure of it, he could read her so vividly.

Others were listening; remember, others were listening.

"How will this help him, Belle?"

"I can save him from being hanged."

"Can you?" He was surprised now by his own calm. "Don't you mean you can save him from being hanged for Cyril's murder? Do you know what else might happen? Can you be sure that having killed once, he will never kill again? What do you want for him, Belle? Happiness? How happy do you think he has been? How long do you want him to live as he did in those last few days at home? Are you sure this is the way to help?" He paused again, and then went on very quietly: "And isn't it time you came to me? Tell me, Belle, do you really think that I deserve all this? Do you hate me so much?"

That hurt her.

"Don't talk like that!"

"But I have to know," Canning insisted. "I have to know why you changed, why you turned to hatred. What had I done? Do you really think that you owe me nothing?"

The tears were at her eyes again.

"George—"

"Just tell me why," Canning said. "Isn't that the least you can do?"

She said: "You will be better off without me. You don't need me, you haven't needed me for years. I've been a burden, and don't pretend that it isn't true. Don't pretend with me now, George, you've always been—so honest, haven't you?" It wasn't a sneer; it was said more in wonderment, but she had told him something else, something he hadn't dreamed of. It made him fight against a surging excitement.

"I've told you there were times I didn't think I could stand for it another day," he reminded her. "A burden? You've been a curse! But—can't curses be lifted? Get this into your head, Belle, I want you desperately. I want to try again."

"You can't want to!"

"It's true," Canning said simply; and exaltation was with him again, he had never felt a surging buoyancy like this. "You're wrong—again. This isn't a way of freeing me. Letting yourself be hanged will leave me—hopeless. At least I've had hope for company in the past."

She said slowly: "It's unbelievable."

"Belle, I thought you were keeping silent to save Bob. That was crazy enough. But to let them hang you because you want to leave me free, to behave like this from some perverted thought of paying for past sins"—he caught his breath, then suddenly smiled at her, and did not know that there was radiance in his eyes. "It's a crazier thing than *I'd* do, Belle! I've taught you self-denial after all." He paused again. "So that's the reason. All your repentance in one heroic deed. Save Bob, free me."

She didn't speak.

"Did you know what he was doing with that sauce?" Canning asked. He went to her, put his hands on her shoulders and let them rest there. "Is that the guilt?"

"No," she said.

"I've tried to tell myself that it was in your mind all the time, that you were just fooling me, but I couldn't believe it. What did happen to you, what made you change towards him?"

She said: "I saw him as he was, and you as you were, and I hated myself. But I still had to try to save him. I couldn't help myself. I fought against seeing it your way. There were times when I thought I could let you tell the police, when I meant to. At others, I knew that I couldn't do it. I promised him I would talk you round. Even when that other boy came, I promised Bob I'd find the money to keep him quiet. I was twisting and turning all the time,

George, but I'd stopped wanting to hurt you. And I did not try to kill you, George. You can believe that."

Everything Canning wanted to know, he knew.

The exaltation carried him above thought of everything else; of practical things. There was beauty in her. She stood up slowly, and he went towards her. They stood together for a long time, and while he was close to her, other, ominous thoughts came into his mind. *He* knew; but that wasn't enough. Her innocence had to be proved. Could it be? There were no other witnesses, no one else who could help. If she were to be saved, she would have to save herself, or Bob had to rescue her.

There was no hope from their son.

He eased her away from him.

"It's been a long time," he said. "I haven't felt like this for—" he didn't finish, her slight, hurt smile stopped him. "Belle—"

"Yes?"

"You'll tell—us—exactly—what you can, won't you? You won't spoil it, now. You'll tell—the police—anything that might save you."

After a long pause, she said: "You mean, will I save myself by condemning him?"

"There isn't any other way," Canning said.

Neither of them moved, but the exaltation had gone, and fear crept back. Could she bring herself to do that? Could she fight back the habit and the yearning of years? Could she turn against Bob? As he watched, Canning felt the old stabbing fear, that it was asking too much of her, too much of any woman.

Then there must be another way.

She spoke at last.

"Even if I would, could I? I didn't see what happened. As far as I know he used the—the root I gave him. You don't have to make me save myself by damning him."

Would she, if she could?

"You can tell the truth, swear that you knew nothing. The jury isn't made up of fools," Canning said tensely.

"*Make* them believe that you had no idea what was in that sauce. You'll have the best lawyers we can get, but—but you'll have to go on with it once you've started. If you're innocent, he must be guilty. Will you defend yourself, Belle?"

After a long time, she said: "Think about it yourself, George. *Can* I help you to drive him to the gallows? *Can* I save myself at his expense? Or even try? What should I feel like, afterwards? I think it would drive me mad," she added abruptly, and turned away from him.

He knew that she would say nothing in her own defence.

24

TRIAL AND TRUTH

THE Court was hushed.

Twelve members of the jury, nine men and three women, sat and watched the Counsel for the Prosecution as tensely as the packed crowd in the public gallery. The Judge, bewigged and placid, listened with a detached interest, as he had throughout the trial. Canning, who had not been called, had been here every moment and sat now with sinking hope, a sense of disaster filling him. Somewhere in the Court was Matthew, who had not been called; the Prosecution had what witnesses it needed. But Celia had been through an ordeal that still made Canning writhe. Weston sat among the reporters in the Press Gallery, next to Randall, who had covered the case himself. Banfield, his red face toned down by the subdued light in the oak-panelled courtroom, looked everywhere but at Canning. And Canning watched his wife.

She had sat quiet, pale and impassive, throughout the trial. But it was possible to sit and listen, and to fancy that he could hear the screeched denials from Bob; to hear his cries and see his tears. He sat tearful now, his eyes enormous, his body trembling. Nothing had given him courage, he had made a complete surrender to fear.

"I didn't do it. I didn't know it was monkshood, I didn't do it!"

Canning could not close his ears to the cries. The fear in him was different, now; that Bob would escape and that Belle would be condemned. He knew that Merrydew had seen that possibility.

Merrydew sat behind the Counsel for the Defence and occasionally leaned over his shoulder, a brown monkey of a man to a lanky eagle of a man. He was doing his best, but what witnesses could they find for the defence? It had been bad enough before; now the prosecuting counsel's deadly work was done. Could anyone be in doubt? All the sickening, sordid story, all the misery of his home life had been brought skilfully before the notice of the jury, so that their minds would be receptive to the final plea. The story of Bob's burglary, the struggle, his flight, was added, too; there was nothing good.

The barrister paused, turned towards the Judge, then gripped his gown up by his neck, and said in his smooth, fluent voice:

"You have, then, the evidence of many witnesses, reliable men and women who have told the simple truth, some with distress, all under solemn oath. You have seen into the minds of this unhappy woman and her unworthy son. They wished death upon any who could, as they believed, bring death to one of themselves. They had the means. You have heard how the difference between the two roots, one edible, one a deadly poison, was demonstrated to them by one of their victims, a demonstration which could hardly be forgotten. I believe, ladies and gentlemen of the jury, that their guilt is proved beyond the slightest shadow of doubt."

He sat down.

For a few moments there was not even a rustle of movement; then many stirred. Bob stared at the man, his lips working; Canning hated the sight of the pale face. He hated the prosecuting counsel for the calm, remorseless way in which he had unfolded facts, for delivering the death blow. What could the defence do? Fussy Merrydew, nervous under the strain, and the tall, beak-nosed barrister with a reputation second to none—but in Canning's experience, nothing to support it. They had met several times; the barrister had been brief, almost brusque.

Now he stood up, hitched up his gown and began to speak in a clear but high-pitched voice, itself surely a disadvantage. But what could the greatest advocate in the world do, now?

Belle watched this man with mild interest.

"M'lud," said Counsel, "this has been a complex case, a long one—yes, I think we must agree that learned counsel has made a *lengthy* business of his task"—the fool, didn't he know that sneering at the prosecution would harden the jury; and weren't they hard enough already?—"and quite understandably, no doubt, all the evidence being circumstantial. But weighty, yes, weighty, heavy enough in fact to weigh the scales of justice down further, perhaps, on the side of *in*justice than has ever happened in my experience. However, I am happy to inform you, m'lud, and you"—he turned round almost casually—"ladies and gentlemen of the jury, that justice, although blind, is not easily fooled and will not be in this case. *Cert*—ainly not. My learned friend, very properly no doubt, wished to establish in the minds of the jury the—ah—somewhat feckless career of the younger of the two accused. With your permission, m'lud, I would like to recall the Chief Witness for the police, Superintendent—ah—Superintendent Edward Banfield."

Banfield was obviously surprised; so was the rest of the Court. Canning, after a moment almost of hope, sank back into depression. How could Banfield help? Would anyone doubt his honesty?

He took the oath.

"M'lud," said Counsel, "with your permission I wish to ask questions relating to the accused's past." His voice was reedy and unimpressive. "Superintendent, will you tell the Court whether, during the past four years, the accused,

Robert George Canning, has been five times summoned and convicted for driving a motor cycle dangerously, to wit, that he ignored the red light of the automatic signals, those happy inventions which relieve your officers of so much patient work—yes?"

Whatever else, he had taken some of the tension out of the atmosphere; two jurors actually smiled.

"He has," Banfield said; he could not hide his surprise.

"There is no doubt or question in your mind that the offences were identical—that he drove past a *red* light without heeding it on each of five occasions?"

Canning thought: "What on earth is he doing? Making the boy out to be a habitual law-breaker?"

"I'm quite satisfied that the evidence was clear," Banfield said.

"I confess," said Counsel, tossing the jury a casual glance, "that I have been most favourably impressed by the carefulness, the thoroughness, the determination of the police in this trying but oh, this so misleading case. You are sure, then, that Robert George Canning on five separate occasions, passed a *red* light. A very careless thing to do. Once understandably, in youthful daring, yes. Twice—a little extra folly, conceivable. But *five* times—three of them after he had been punished for an identical offence, when he must have known that every policeman in the vicinity, doubtless on the implicit instructions of the Chief Superintendent, was looking out for him to err again. It makes the accused a greater fool than most of us would agree. I think. *Five* times." The Judge looked as if he were going to stop this speech-making, and learned Counsel's tone changed. "Thank you, Superintendent."

Canning looked at the Counsel's beak of a nose and the impassive face beneath the wig, and found his heart beating fast. What did this mean? How could it help? He saw no way, but the confidence of the barrister drove hope into him. There was a difference in the expressions of the jury, too; eagerness.

"Now, m'lud, I would like to call a young lady, a most

charming young lady and, I confess, a friend of the accused. At least, a friend at one time. Miss Lucy Worrell."

Canning had never heard of her. Lucy Worrell?

She came, a little, high-breasted girl of nineteen, or twenty, nicely made-up, neatly dressed in a grey suit, obviously nervous. Swearing the oath, she was barely audible. Counsel nursed her cleverly; this man was *good*.

She had known Bob for some time, she had been 'his girl', he had cooled off, they had not gone out together for several months. *Where was this leading to?* How did the accused, Robert Canning, take her out?

"Why, sir, on his motor-bike."

"On what part of his motor-bike?"

"Why, the pillion."

"Thank you. Did he always stop when he saw a red light—a traffic light?"

"Well—no. Once or twice he passed them."

"Thank you. I—m'lud." Counsel swung round. "I do assure you that these questions, while appearing irrelevant, will have a very important bearing upon the decision of the jury, and upon the rights and wrongs of his trial. Miss Worrell, I would like you to tell the Judge and jury exactly what Robert Canning said, when the police had finished on that occasion. Not—ah—perhaps the *precise* words which showed his opinion of the police—" he paused; and several members of the jury smiled; tension had gone. *But this was for Bob, not Belle. Belle had to be saved!* "What was his comment, Miss Worrell?"

"He said he didn't notice the signals."

"Where exactly did this incident occur?"

"Why, at the junction of High Street and Bath Road."

"Whereabouts in Minchester is that?"

"Why, bang in the middle!"

"The accused certainly knew that there were traffic lights at that spot; I think we can safely say that, for he has spent his life in or near Minchester," said Counsel readily. "Yet he said that he did not notice the signals. Is that everything he said?"

"Well—" she hesitated. "I remember ever so well, he said he didn't notice the damned thing was red."

"Had you noticed it change?"

"Well—"

"Don't be afraid to tell the simple truth, Miss Worrell, that is all I ask of you. Did you see that the light was red at the time?"

"Well, actually, I did."

"Thank you," said Counsel briskly. "That is all." This was the time for the prosecution to question her; they made no attempt. Canning sat bewildered, and the rest of the Court was equally puzzled. "M'lud," said Counsel abruptly, "I am going to call the accused, Robert George Canning—with your permission, m'lud."

This was dreadful. Bob in the witness box would be disastrous; from the moment his name was called he began to tremble. Two warders and a policeman helped him, he almost needed carrying.

"Robert," Counsel said in a dry, hurried voice, "I propose with your help to show to the jury that you are completely innocent of the crime of which you are accused. I shall not keep you long. M'lud, the Prosecution, rightly, no doubt, made great play of a demonstration of the differences between two roots, one poisonous, the other edible. I crave your indulgence for another, very brief demonstration. Robert." he swung round on Bob; he was keeping him as steady as anyone could. He picked up a manilla folder, and took out of it a sheet of white paper; "what colour is that?"

"W—w—white," Bob stammered.

What was the man getting at?

"Thank you." Counsel put the white paper down, picked up a sheet of bright violet. "What colour is that?"

"It—it—it's blue."

Blue? Anyone could see that it was violet.

"Thank you." Counsel picked up a sheet of bright orange paper. "What colour is that?"

Bob stared at it, open-mouthed, and didn't speak.

"Don't worry, this isn't a trick, it will simply prove your

innocence," Counsel said soothingly. "Don't pretend, don't lie. What colour is it?"

"It's—it's green!"

Green? Nonsense, it was bright orange.

"Thank you, Just one more." Counsel snatched a piece of crimson cloth from the folder, and held it up, waving it as a red rag to a bull. "The colour, please, quickly. Quickly!"

"Green!" screamed Bob.

Then silence fell.

There were other witnesses, including experts on colour blindness, who said how it could be acquired, how many people did not even suspect that they were colour blind. It was established beyond reasonable doubt that Bob could not have seen the pink on the monkshood root.

. . . . .

"The Prosecution thought that the accused Robert Canning had seen the pink stain which comes from the juice or sap of a monkshood root when cut, and believed that he would, therefore, know that he was preparing a poisonous dish on the day of the death of Cyril Rigby," Counsel said. "In fact he could not tell any difference in colour. But he did prepare the fatal sauce. He selected the root; his mother simply told him to take one out of a box. You have heard him say so, very clearly. He did not know that it was monkshood. May I trespass upon the indulgence of the Court and suggest that even his father, very familiar with the pinky tinge of monkshood sap, did not notice that the prepared sauce was also slightly tinged pink—because it was a dull, grey day, and light was poor. A man with good normal eyesight, then, noticed nothing.

"Now, about the other accused, Mrs. Canning. As she did not pick up this particular root and place it in her son's hand, how can there be any suspicion that she knew what was being done? We have seen the box—in court. There is one other monkshood root in it, the rest are horseradish.

"Ladies and gentlemen, I shall not detain you any longer," Counsel went on. "This is not a case of murder but of accidental death. The accused, Robert Canning, may have made mistakes, but that does not make him a murderer. The accused, Belle Eileen Canning, has refused to speak, to say a single word to save herself, and for what reason? She believed that it would condemn her son to the gallows. What greater love can a mother have than this, which would have sent her willingly to the gallows to save her own son? M'lud, with respect, I submit that there should have been no indictment in this case."

He sat down.

Canning could not see him, or the Judge or the jury; or Bob or any others there. He could see only Belle, as she looked towards him, her hands held out as if she were waiting for him to go and take them.

They had to sit through the formalities. The jury retired for twenty minutes, but Canning was not even in suspense while he waited for the foreman's *Not Guilty*.

25

REST

CANNING felt at ease, comfortable in his armchair, with the day's work finished and on the desk, where he would pack and post it to London. Belle would walk with him down to the post-box. She was in the garden, shifting the hose which was spraying the vegetables, rescuing them from the weeks of dry weather which had lasted through May and June and half-way through July. Yet it was not really a hot summer; just comfortable.

There had been no real tension during the day, only a little constraint. They had talked about the cause of this for a while after breakfast, not pretended that there was none. The Assizes were in session at Minchester again. Bob was on trial for the burglary at the Dales' house. In the same court, when that was over, Jerry Dale would be on trial for his life.

Merrydew had looked after Bob's interests; several other charges had been included, once Merrydew had persuaded Bob to admit to them. The verdict was in no doubt, the only uncertainty was the sentence.

Canning heard Belle come in.

She called up: "Like a cup of tea, darling?"

"I'll come down."

"Five minutes," she called.

He didn't get up immediately. It was easy to rest. There was no longer any strain or struggle. Who could wonder that Belle was subdued and quiet at times?

They all helped her. Celia, who was here two or three times a week, Matthew who looked in most week-ends and occasionally in the evening. They had a flat in Minchester, near his office. They had gone to the trial to-day. Canning had asked Belle if she wanted to go, but she had said 'no'; and he did not think that she wished she had gone.

He stood up.

The telephone bell rang.

He reached for it quickly, heart in mouth. He heard Belle fly along the hall towards the instrument downstairs.

"This is George Canning."

"Hallo, Dad," said Matthew, "it's just finished. It could have been worse—three years." The sound on the line was the gasp from Belle, downstairs. "He put up a much better show in the dock," Matthew went on. "I won't stop now, Celia and I will be out right away. Good-bye."

He rang off.

Canning could not get downstairs quickly enough, but there was no need to worry. Belle had put the receiver down, and was waiting for him. She did not smile; nor did she cry.

"It could make him," Canning said heavily.

"Yes, I suppose it could," Belle's voice was dry, without emotion. "I don't think we ought to expect too much, though, his life wasn't at stake this time. It's all right, darling, I'm not being bitter, I'm just accepting facts. I suppose I made him what he is." She looked into Canning's eyes, candidly, calmly. "I've not been sure how I should feel when it really happened, but there's nothing to worry about. Bob can't really hurt me any more. The strange thing is that when I was carrying him, I thought I should hate the touch and sight of him. I had to wait until now, to tell you why. I was going to leave you, George—eighteen months after Celia was born. I met another man. We were going to live together. He would have married me as soon as I was free." She was still quiet-voiced, unemotional "Then I discovered that Bob was coming. It nearly drove me mad. But then he—my lover—died. No, Bob wasn't his child, he was ours. I'd tell you if he weren't. So I was left with a grief I couldn't share, and I began to—to hate you."

"Belle—" Canning began hoarsely.

"You had to know," Belle said, and stopped him from speaking with a gesture. "There were times when I thought I would have to leave you, but I could never bring myself to it. I—"

"Belle, be quiet and listen!"

She obeyed.

"We had some good years, many bad ones, and the good have come back," Canning said. "The past is the past. Do you want anything more from the present? Is there anything we can change that you want different?" Before she could answer, he said deliberately: "Because I don't."

She gave no answer, and he needed none. They went together into the kitchen, where the kettle was boiling, and he made the tea while she prepared the tray. Afterwards, they walked to the post-box together and met Celia and Matthew, on the way.

ABOUT THE AUTHOR

John Creasey is a towering figure in the arts of mystery and suspense. The range of his writing, the staggering number of books to his credit, and his ability to write different but equally compelling kinds of stories under each of ten different pen names qualify him as a modern master. Continuing characters like Commander Gideon, Inspector West, Dr. Cellini, the Toff, the Baron, and Dr. Palfrey have become fixtures in the imaginations of readers in every corner of the world.

Mr. Creasey divides his time between his country house in England and his new house in Arizona. Father of a comfortably large family (two sons, as well as a mystery-writer father are the central characters in the now-classic Richard, Martin, and Jonathan Fane series of books), he also finds time for active participation in political action and other interests such as the history of the American West.

For forty years he has poured out an astonishing flood of stories, characters, intricate plots, and strategies, writing from the viewpoint of man and woman with equal verisimilitude; through the eyes of criminal and policeman—and of their families—the young and the old, the rich and the poor, high society and low. Because as an Englishman he cannot "see" as an American, he seldom writes from the viewpoint of an American character, although his pen-pictures of America and Americans are not only vivid but often startlingly true to life. He has crisscrossed all forty-eight of the mainland states by road, and probably knows the country better than anyone not born and bred in it.